Marie Oomen

79

Leaving the place where Heidi and Grandfather had lived for years, Heidi turned to have a last look around the beloved Alm-hut. Seeing the colorful rug by the fireplace, she ran over and carefully folded it before putting it on her grandfather's rocker. Picking up her basket, she joined her cousins outside, locking the door behind her and placing the key in a secret place behind a little bush. The party started their journey toward Dörfli. The fir trees sang sadly in the winter winds.

JOHN PEARSON spent more than twenty years as a Heidi enthusiast and a student of the life of Johanna Spyri. It was his original idea to update the classic _Heidi_ and bring it to the screen. Born in England, Mr. Pearson served with British forces in World War II and has been a poet, writer, director, and actor. He now lives with his wife, Barbara, in Beverly Hills, California, where he is president of John Pearson International, a television company.

THE LAUREL-LEAF LIBRARY brings together under a single imprint outstanding works of fiction and non-fiction particularly suitable for young adult readers, both in and out of the classroom. The series is under the editorship of Charles F. Reasoner, Professor of Elementary Education, New York University.

THE NEW ADVENTURES OF HEIDI

A novel by
JOHN PEARSON

From the NBC Motion Picture
THE NEW ADVENTURES OF HEIDI

Produced by
PIERRE COSSETTE PRODUCTIONS

In association with
MAX APPELBOOM PRODUCTIES, B.V.

Written by
JOHN McGREEVEY

Based on characters created by
JOHANNA SPYRI

From the original novel
HEIDI

Title and Generic Concept by
JOHN PEARSON

Published by
Dell Publishing Co., Inc.
1 Dag Hammarskjold Plaza
New York, New York 10017

Laurel-Leaf ® TM 766734 Dell Publishing Co., Inc.

ISBN: 0-440-96846-1

Printed in the United States of America

First Laurel-Leaf printing—December 1978

DEDICATED TO BARBARA—
WITH ALL MY LOVE

My sincere thanks for all their help
and encouragement to—
Max, Lena, Ken, Pierre, John,
Arnie, Hans, Cliff, & Lee

And in special memory of "Hanni,"
without whose inspiration, genius, and sensitivity
"HEIDI" would never have existed.

CONTENTS

Chapter I
THE ALM-HUT

The old town of Maienfeld, in the Swiss canton of Grisons, lies above the valley of the Rhine, sheltered by mountains. Way above the little town to the north is the magnificent Falknis, or falcon's nest, its highest peaks wrapped in cloud, though on this late summer day the valley basked in sunshine. Beyond the Falknis lie the Liechtenstein mountains, and farther north the Vorarlberg guards the Swiss-Austrian frontier. To the northwest of Maienfeld the heights of Fläschenberg assist the Falknis in guarding the road to Liechtenstein, for in the old days this road was the only gateway to Austria, which for many years was the archenemy of the Swiss. But that was long, long ago, and now the countries of Switzerland, Austria and Liechtenstein live together as the friendliest of neighbors. And peace best describes this valley of the Rhine. It's true that in the valley below an autobahn has been built connecting Zurich with Chur and the Alpine resorts of Davos and Arosa, and one can see from the vineyards surrounding Maienfeld the busy traffic in the distance. But one cannot hear

the traffic's roar. The only sounds are the distant
tinkling of bells from grazing goats and cattle from
the lush green mountain slopes. Beside the autobahn the Rhine can be seen glistening in the sun,
but in this part of the valley it is a narrow Alpine
river that rises in the south of this same canton of
Grisons.

Above Maienfeld, hidden by clusters of fir trees,
is the village of Dörfli, which to the Swiss means
"Little Village."

Dörfli is so small a village that it's not on any
map, but the villagers are friendly, and if you wander upon it one day, they will be proud to show
you their little school and the old gasthaus, or inn,
the Alpenrose, in the tiny main street. Farther up
the slopes above Dörfli are steep meadows bearing
rich grass and summer flowers of all colors, blue
gentians, white daisies and red clover. The Swiss
call these flowers enzian, margrite and klee. The
meadows seem to rise to the sky, but nearer the
summit of the mountains the ground becomes
rocky, and clumps of fir trees scatter the upper
slopes.

On one of the higher meadows a young girl and
boy were playing, surrounded by a herd of goats.
The girl, who looked about ten years old, was
sturdy, with beautiful light-colored hair that shone
in the sun. Her skin was tanned by the Alpine air,
and her whole being seemed to radiate health.
With rosy cheeks and deep blue eyes, her expres-
sive face constantly broke into a smile, and her in-
fectious laugh blended with the tinkle of the bells

on the goats' necks. Although dressed in plain country clothes and barefooted, as she had taken off her shoes to play, in these idyllic surroundings she seemed like a little Alpine princess. She wore an air of gaiety and charm. Her name was Heidi.

Her companion, in contrast to Heidi's good spirits, was frowning. Of about the same age, he was tall and slim. One might say he was almost gangly, as if his body were striving towards a manhood beyond his years. Despite his thin frame, he was powerful for a boy of his age, with a wiry strength developed by climbing mountain slopes and tending his herd of goats.

"Peter, you don't know how funny you look," laughed Heidi. Peter was not amused, as at this moment he was engaged in a tug-of-war with one of the more stubborn goats.

"Get back, Bärli—you stubborn old devil," shouted Peter. The large brown and white goat was named Bärli, meaning "Little Bear," but Peter thought there was nothing bearlike about him.

Heidi shook her head, still smiling. "Bärli doesn't know what you want him to do."

Bärli strained at the rope.

"Wave your apron at him, Heidi," called Peter in desperation. Heidi obliged, and Bärli responded by moving back in the other direction. Now the rope between him and Peter was taut again.

"That's it," said Peter, "don't stop. Wave your apron some more."

Heidi obediently waved her apron, and the old rope snapped under the strain, making Peter fall over backwards. Heidi, seeing that only Peter's dignity was hurt, burst into laughter. Bärli joined in the fun by baaing raucously. Peter got to his feet, brushing himself off.

"Go on, laugh," he said. "But just wait till I'm the champion athlete in Maienfeld."

Heidi was still chuckling. "Maybe Bärli will be the champion if he keeps practicing." Heidi's and Peter's eyes met, and a weak smile crossed Peter's face. Then they looked to the sky above the far mountains, with Heidi shielding her eyes against the glare. In the deep-blue distance, above the snow-topped peaks, could be seen a thin silver vapor trail. Then farther to the right, they could just make out the tiny birdlike form of a jetliner as it disappeared into the clouds.

Heidi looked down the mountainside.

"Maybe we'd better be going back," she said. Heidi moved towards Bärli to loosen the snapped rope on his neck. Behind Bärli was a cluster of rocks. Heidi had a sudden feeling that someone was in the rocks and watching them. She turned to Peter, at the same time nodding toward the rocks. She whispered, "Peter—there's somebody—"

As they looked towards the rocks, there was a scrabbling sound of loose gravel. Peter dashed towards the sound. As he did so, a weird-looking figure burst from behind the boulders and in a strange loping run made for a chasm in the rocks and disappeared. The move was so sudden and unexpected that neither of them had time to form a clear picture of the strange being. Their only impression was of what they assumed to be a man with long hair and a ragged covering of some sort. Peter dashed towards the chasm.

"Peter—come back. You can't catch him. Peter—" Heidi called after him. But Peter continued the chase. The strange figure suddenly appeared again, leaping from the edge of the chasm to a rock below and then to another rock, for all the world like a wild long-haired mountain goat. Peter reached the edge of the cliff and stared down, but no one was in sight. The stranger had vanished in the lengthening shadows. Heidi ran to catch up with Peter. Both stared into the darkening rocky slopes.

"That's the second time we've seen the wildenmann this week." Heidi was not frightened, but her voice trembled.

"Someday I'll track him down," muttered Peter grimly.

"Grandfather says men have tried to follow him for years."

"I'm going to be the one who does it," exclaimed Peter bravely.

"Before or after you become champion athlete?" asked Heidi, laughing again.

The goats, during the past minutes of excitement, had straggled and were baaing frantically. Peter forgot his short-lived irritation at Heidi's last comment and with a whistle gathered the goat herd together. He and Heidi then started their return journey down the mountainside, with the goats following in single file.

After carefully descending for perhaps half an hour, they reached a simple cottage, protected from the winds by tall fir trees. Beyond the trees was a shed and shelter used for housing animals. Chickens, ducks, geese and rabbits were all kept in and around the shed—not to mention Heidi's two pet goats, Bärli and Schwänli. For this was Heidi's grandfather's cottage, and the animals belonged to him, together with a number of strays that Heidi constantly added.

As Heidi and Peter approached, Grandfather was standing near the shed peering into the valley in the growing twilight. He was a tall, handsome man, with white hair and beard. His face was gnarled and weather-beaten, and his fine features might have been carved out of teak. Wilhelm Beck had, according to the stories told in Dörfli, led a strange life. Born in the Grisons, in his younger days he had been a prosperous farmer. But then, according to the villagers, he had disappeared. That was before the war, and no one in the village heard of him for many years. There were rumors, of course. Some of tragedy and some of scandal. But no one knew for sure. And then after the war, Wilhelm Beck arrived back in Dörfli, bringing with him a small boy, who he told the village was his son. But not one word more as to where he had been all those years or where his wife was, if he had a wife.

The boy, Bernhard, grew up and prospered in the village, being apprenticed to a local lumber merchant. When Bernhard became a man, he took over the lumber business and married Adelheid, a girl from a nearby village. Bernhard and his wife had one child, a beautiful little girl whom they called Heidi. But tragedy hit the Beck family. Bernhard was killed in an accident at the lumber works, and Adelheid mysteriously died soon after, of a broken heart they said in Dörfli. At about that time, Grandfather Beck seemed to turn his back on the world and left the village to build his cottage far up the mountain. Heidi was taken in for a short while by her Aunt Gritli, who worked in an embroidery near Bad Ragaz. But before long Heidi yearned to see her grandfather again, and Gritli persuaded Wilhelm Beck to take the child, as she was being transferred to another embroidery in St. Gallen. And so a year or so ago Heidi joined her grandfather in what the villagers called the Alm-hut. Although the people of Dörfli usually addressed Wilhelm Beck as Wilhelm or Herr Beck, they often referred to him as the Alm-Uncle. Because through the years, in a small village such as Dörfli so many inhabitants were related either by marriage or as distant cousins, the term "Alm-Uncle" was recognized by everyone and was considered a friendly and almost affectionate name. So all in Dörfli knew of their own little Heidi and how she lived happily up the mountain with Alm-Uncle in the cottage known as the Alm-hut.

Grandfather spoke. His voice was deep and rich in country dialect, yet there was a softness there that hinted of travel or perhaps the passing of long years of solitude and meditation. A gruff tone with a hint of weariness was in his words.

"So, General—how went the battle today?" He looked at Peter.

"Another glorious victory," said Heidi, smiling, taking Grandfather's hand. Her reply was a daily joke between them, as Grandfather always looked on the mountain trek with the goats as a military operation. He had that rare quality and wisdom of never talking down to children, treating Heidi and Peter as equals, yet never forgetting his ultimate authority as the old Alm-Uncle. Grandfather and Heidi urged Bärli and Schwänli towards the shed, and Peter herded the other goats together, preparing for his further descent of the mountain to his father's farm.

"The troops seem in good spirits," said Grandfather, "except the old sergeant here." He patted Bärli.

"Oh, that one," retorted Peter. "He goes forwards when I want him to go backwards and backwards when I want him to go forwards. He's part mule."

Heidi chortled. "And part pig. We should send him to the Zurich zoo."

Peter called the other goats by name, as though encouraging the tired animals for the last part of their trip home. "Come on, Schnecke. Won't be long now, Big Turk." Schnecke moved slowly, as his name of snail implied. Big Turk was the oldest, wisest and most unruly of the herd. By nature he was a fighter, but Peter kept a strict eye on this one. The others, Schneehöpli, or Little Snowhopper, and Distelfinck, The Goldfinch, followed obediently behind Big Turk, keeping a safe distance, as they knew of Big Turk's bad temper, particularly at the end of the day.

"See you in the morning," Peter called to Heidi and her grandfather.

"Don't get lost on your way home, General," said Grandfather.

Peter tapped his pocket. "Not with my compass."

"Don't worry," smiled Heidi. "The goats lead him home." The little caravan set off down the mountain in single file, with Peter leading and Schneehöpli, still skipping despite the late hour, bringing up the rear.

Heidi and Grandfather led their two goats into the shed, preparing to bed them down for the night. Heidi checked their water while her grandfather raked the straw.

"Grandfather, we saw the wild man again today."

The old man straightened his back and, without turning his head, spoke slowly. There was a tone of concern in his voice.

"Maybe you shouldn't go up there with the goats."

Heidi, who had filled the water pail, spoke quietly.

"He never really bothers anybody—" Heidi was almost defensive about the strange figure up in the rocky heights.

Grandfather seemed almost to be talking to himself. "Umm." He paused a moment in thought. "And nobody bothers him. I once lived that kind of life." The old man turned slowly and looked at Heidi, nodding, then he resumed his raking.

Their work in the shed finished, the couple returned to the Alm-hut, Heidi holding her grandfather's hand.

Inside the cottage, Grandfather collected his pipe and tobacco pouch from the table and settled himself in the rocking chair by the fireplace. Heidi was always relieved when her grandfather lit his pipe rather than one of those thin crooked cigars that he sometimes bought from the store in Dörfli. But she never complained and was always happy to see her grandfather relaxed and puffing his old carved pipe as he rocked gently in his favorite chair. Heidi busied herself with setting the table.

Grandfather always referred to the room as "the stube," which was what the villagers called their living room, yet at the Alm-hut this was the only room, with the exception of the loft, which served as Heidi's bedroom and was reached by a handsome carved wooden ladder. The stube was neat and clean, with solid handmade furniture of shiny well-worn pine and fir. The table, with two chairs, one considerably larger than the other, was in the center of the room and was covered with a dark green cloth. Heidi, when she looked at the table with the two chairs always secretly thought of the story her Aunt Gritli had told her of *The Three*

Bears, with their different-sized chairs and bowls. But we're only two bears she laughed to herself, and I'm the Little Bear.

Between puffs on his pipe, Grandfather spoke slowly. "Peter seemed in low spirits today. No jokes."

"He's thinking about school," Heidi replied.

"Oh, school," muttered Grandfather. With a slight shiver, as though he felt a draft from the coming autumn, he rose and poked the logs in the fire. Clouds of sparks rose up the old chimney. Grandfather always made a fire later in the day, even before autumn, as the mountain air was cool at night and he did not want Heidi to catch cold after her day up the mountain.

Grandfather straightened his back, and was standing by the fireplace.

"The summer's gone by so soon. The days fly quickly." He paused. "When does school begin?"

"Monday, Grandfather."

Grandfather bent to poke the fire once more, then, standing, reached for the rocking chair. His hand quivering, he clutched the chair for support. The room was blurred and even the smoldering fire logs were dim.

Heidi, returning from the kitchen, saw the old man pass his hand wearily across his eyes.

"Grandfather—?"

"If the table's set, let's eat," muttered the old man almost testily. Heidi fetched the pitcher of goat's milk and, while setting it on the table, watched her grandfather out of the corner of her eye. Grandfather was now gripping the fireplace and again wiped his eyes. Then he steadied him self. Heidi poured the milk into two glasses. Not a Big Bear's glass and a Little Bear's glass, she thought. They're both the same size. For Heidi loved the goat's milk she had drunk every day since arriving at the Alm-hut.

"Are you sure you're all right?" she asked, a her grandfather moved slowly to the table and sat down. Grandfather nodded, bowing his head in prayer. Heidi followed, placing her hands together as Grandfather said grace.

"Thank you, God, for this food and all your other kindness. Help us to be grateful for life's blessings and to accept our disappointments with out complaint or bitterness. Amen."

They both raised their heads. Heidi looked straight at her grandfather, her eyes wondering There seemed to be a question on her face. Grand father avoided her gaze, and picked up his bread and cheese.

"Eat your supper," he said.

Heidi obediently took a long drink of the sweet goat's milk and helped herself to a piece of bread She still wore a look of concern.

There was silence, save for an occasional clink of glasses or knives on plates and the crackle from the log fire.

Grandfather and Heidi finished their meal with out a word spoken. . . .

Later that night, though Heidi had gone to bed several hours earlier, Grandfather was sitting in his chair, gently rocking and staring at the still-glowing embers. After a while, he rose slowly and quietly climbed the ladder to the loft. He looked down at the little girl sleeping peacefully in the big bed that he had made for her when she first arrived at the Alm-hut. As he watched the sleeping child, a tremendous sense of grief and loss seemed to overwhelm him. Recovering his composure, he reached down and tucked in the quilt. Heidi moved slightly, then with a long sigh returned to deep sleep.

Grandfather quietly climbed down the ladder, washed his face at the kitchen sink and silently crept into bed.

Soon the Alm-hut was sleeping. The still of the night was broken only by occasional heavy breathing and the murmur of the wind in the firs.

Chapter II
THE ALPENROSE—
NO ROOM FOR A CHILD

In Dörfli the morning sun shone brightly, yet there was an unmistakable air of early autumn. Small clusters of leaves danced down the main street, and old men were tending to the log piles behind their houses, preparing for the winter cold only a month or so away. The street seemed busier than usual. A few villagers were returning to their houses carrying bottles and containers of milk bought from the co-op van that stopped every morning outside the post office.

Small groups of children with leather satchels on their backs walked slowly, their feet dragging towards the schoolhouse.

Doors opened and little heads peered down the street, as though they were delaying to the last minute the end of their summer holidays. The school bell was ringing, a summons they could not ignore. Apart from the little schoolhouse, there were few buildings in the tiny street. The village church stood solidly on the crossroads of the road to Maienfeld, and a few steps away the second most important gathering point in the little village,

their own gasthaus, The Alpenrose. Then next to
the gasthaus, the general store, and two doors
away, the cobbler's shop. Boots and shoes were
important in this mountain village, and no one
would dream of going to Maienfeld or elsewhere to
buy them if they could be found at Hans Baumes,
where there was such a wonderful smell of old
leather and polish. Besides, Herr Baumes was almost a figurehead in the village, being both police
officer and Burgermeister.

On this morning, Grandfather, Heidi and Peter
came down the path to the village from the Alm-
hut. Grandfather was leaning on his carved and
distinctive alpenstock, and Heidi was clutching
his other hand, almost skipping beside him, in
contrast to the Alm-Uncle's heavy deliberate steps.
Following the couple came Peter, disconsolately
kicking stones from the path, and wearing a frown
that contrasted with Heidi's unconcealed cheer-
fulness. The path from the Alm-hut passed the
farm where Peter lived with his parents, and
Grandfather and Heidi had agreed to collect Peter
on their walk down to the village, otherwise they
were certain he would be late for school.

Heidi looked around at her friend, who appeared
more gangly and loose-limbed than ever this
morning, and seemed most reluctant to keep pace
with them.

"Peter—come on! We don't want to be late the
first day."

"I wish it was the last day," Peter grumbled.
And the two moved on down towards the ringing

bell. As they reached the village street, they were recognized on all sides. "Grützi, Alm-Uncle"; "Grützi, Heidi." "Grützi," they both replied, Heidi smiling at old friends. Everyone seemed to know them, and Heidi remembered almost everybody. As they passed the cobbler's shop, Hans Baumes stepped into the street and greeted them.

"Grützi, Wilhelm. Two sure signs that winter's coming—animals go into their lairs and you come down to Dörfli."

"Only for the day," replied Grandfather, then turning to the children, "I'll wait for you two at the Alpenrose. We'll eat before we start back."

Heidi and Peter, seeing a group of their friends passing, joined them and, after many an exchange of "Grützi," made their way to the schoolhouse.

Grandfather, leaning on his stick, stayed talking with Hans Baumes. "So Hans, how goes it with you?"

"Well, thank God most people wear shoes," said Hans, lighting a small cigar.

"Heidi needs new winter boots," said Grandfather.

"I'll fit her, have no fear. Snug and warm."

"And how about your other duties?" asked Grandfather. "How's the Burgermeister and the police chief?"

Hans Baumes smiled. "Oh, the usual little problems," he replied. "Frau Geiger had one too many the other night. And old Peter Meier let his dog break into the Weber's rabbit hutch."

"You have heavy responsibilities," said Grandfather.

The Burgermeister agreed with a wry grin.

For a moment Grandfather's eyes blurred and the street darkened. He wiped his eyes. But the attack passed quickly.

"Are you all right?" asked Hans, with a hand on the old man's shoulder.

"Fine," replied Grandfather, "just fine."

Hans was a friendly man in his mid-fifties, and he had a soft spot in his heart for Heidi, remembering the day she was born and the joy the little girl brought to her parents, Bernhard and Adelheid. He also remembered the two funerals, both held on grey winter days, when Adelheid was laid beside Bernhard in the little cemetery behind the church. All this passed quickly through his mind as he studied the Alm-Uncle leaning on his stick, staring with misty eyes into the Rhine valley. Yes, Heidi was lucky to be living with the old man, Hans thought. They were both lucky.

Grandfather broke the pause, turning toward Hans. "I have to go to the post office," he said.

"I'll walk with you," suggested Hans, "and maybe afterwards we'll have a glass together at the Alpenrose." The two men walked slowly down the street.

Although the year was waning, today the sun was warm, and at the Alpenrose lunch was served on the small terrace ablaze with geraniums. As even the visiting pastor, who held services every

Sunday at the village church, would probably agree, the Alpenrose was the most popular meeting place for the people of Dörfli. Throughout the day, both young and old men would drop into the cozy bar for a friendly beer. In the afternoon, the more prosperous housewives, their daily chores over, would meet for coffee and "tortli," the delicious cakes baked in the Alpenrose kitchen by the owner's wife. But the evenings were the busiest, and even more so lately, since a small television set had been installed in the main stube. It perhaps seemed out of place to see, on the three-hundred-year-old brick chimney top, a spiderlike aerial reaching towards the sky. Though some wondered how this weird wire contraption could attract pictures out of the air, there were no complaints, but only fevered excitement when it brought them the football games from Zurich, which had to be hundreds of kilometers away across the mountains.

But even the novelty of television would never surpass the popularity of cards at the Alpenrose. Every evening from around eight o'clock till closing time the three tables in the bar would be occupied by card players.

Lingering over drinks or coffee, men of all ages, their pipes or cigars filling the air with an acrid mist, would be lost in concentration. Over the general buzz of background chatter would be heard an occasional shout of triumph as a winning card was slapped down hard onto the table. The more important the player considered his card, the harder he slapped it down. Such a play was greeted with grunts of approval from the onlookers. The evening game of cards, called "jass," was a highlight in the day of many villagers. To an observer the game might appear like the English whist. Although they had in recent years been allowed to vote in elections and were certainly accepted in the bar, women were never seen at the card tables. This was definitely a male preserve and the players intended to keep it that way.

Shortly after twelve o'clock, Grandfather selected a table on the terrace and, having ordered an appenzeller, sipped the reddish-brown drink slowly and gazed down the street. He smiled to himself as he mused over the stories that were told about the people from the northern canton of Appenzell, which was a fine canton; it was just that Of course, there was nothing really strange about Appenzell, which was a fine canton; it was just that the people were small. Grandfather's face again creased with a smile. Just as the British had their Scots jokes, and the Germans told Polish stories, so the Swiss told their tales of Appenzell. Why, the mountain people there were so small that if they jumped off a little stool, they'd break both their legs. Grandfather almost laughed. But then a frown crossed his face, and a feeling of sadness made him forget all about the wee folk of Appenzell, for there were Heidi and Peter hurrying down the street. Quite a change from Peter's lazy manner earlier in the day. The children joined Grandfather at his table.

Heidi was excited and enthusiastic. "We have a new teacher, Grandfather," she bubbled.

"Who talks too much," Peter added. "But she's pretty."

The waitress approached the table. Grandfather ordered. "Fräulein, for the children, schüblig mit rösti."

"Danke schön." The waitress returned to the kitchen.

Heidi looked at Grandfather. "To do our new arithmetic we need a ruler and a protractor. Could we buy them at the store?" she asked.

Grandfather looked straight ahead into the street. He spoke slowly. "You won't be going to school here."

Both Heidi and Peter stared at the old man with a look of dismay. Grandfather, avoiding Heidi's eyes, took an envelope from his pocket. "It's all here," he said. "I have a letter from the Luzern cousins. You remember them?"

Heidi nodded. "Yes—Cousin Tobias and Cousin Martha."

Grandfather continued hesitatingly. "They've agreed you can go and live with them."

"But why, Grandfather—why?" Heidi pleaded.

Grandfather tried to explain. "I have a chance for a good job in Chur. So I'm leaving the Alm, leaving Dörfli."

Heidi and Peter couldn't believe what they were hearing. The waitress had brought their food, but it remained untouched as they stared at the old man in disbelief.

"You never said you wanted to go away from the Alm," exclaimed Heidi.

"At my age, I can't pass up a chance like this." Grandfather spoke haltingly.

"Take me with you," pleaded Heidi.

Grandfather, as though ignoring Heidi's pleas, continued. "I'll be living in the boss's house. There's no room for a child. You'll be much better off in Luzern. You'll go to a fine school. Cousin Martha will teach you the things a girl your age should learn. . . ."

Heidi looked at Peter in dismay, but Peter was dumbfounded.

"Please, Grandfather—?" said Heidi, gulping back tears.

The old man was adamant. "It's settled. You'll live in Luzern."

There was silence for a moment, then Heidi spoke softly.

"When do I have to go?"

"Tomorrow." It was as though a judge was pronouncing a sentence, which greatly troubled him. During the last few moments Heidi's eyes had not left her grandfather's face, and he found her silent appeal almost unbearable.

"Eat your lunch," he said, almost savagely.

Heidi and Peter mechanically obeyed. When they had left school they had agreed they were hungry, and were looking forward to meeting

Grandfather at the Alpenrose. But now they looked down at their plates with little interest and played with their food as their minds tried to absorb the shock of Grandfather's sudden and dramatic announcement.

Chapter III
A CHANGE IN PLANS

The return journey to the Alm-hut seemed longer and more tiring than ever before. Grandfather walked slowly but determinedly several paces in front of Heidi and Peter who hardly spoke to each other. When they reached Peter's farm, Peter whispered "wiedersehn" to Heidi and slipped through the iron gate without another word. Grandfather, looking straight ahead, hardly acknowledged that Peter left and continued his climb, mechanically jabbing his old carved stick into the upward path. Heidi followed him, every now and then looking up at the back of the old man's head with a puzzled yet resigned expression. As they approached the hut, a dark cloud covered the sun, and Heidi's waning spirits seemed to fall further, increasing the strain between them.

When they reached the yard fence surrounding the shed, the sound of the chickens and goats seemed more plaintive than usual. The old man moved towards the hut porch, and Heidi stopped, looking towards the shed. She called to her grandfather, now standing at the door of the hut with his back to her.

"If you go to Chur, and I go to Luzern, what will happen to—" Heidi was listening to the animals. Grandfather turned and there was a touch of finality in the old voice.

"It's all been taken care of," he said, entering the hut. Heidi paused, then walked to the shed, her steps quickening. Inside she looked slowly round at all her friends and then, with a little shrug of her shoulders, as if by habit went through her daily routine of scattering grain for the chickens, filling up the water containers, and finding her pet rabbit a fresh lettuce leaf. Bärli stopped drinking and, turning his head, looked up at Heidi with his plaintive old eyes. Heidi impulsively threw her arms around Bärli, giving him a long and extra-loving hug.

When her chores were finished, she returned to the hut, where her grandfather was sitting in his usual chair, rocking gently. He was looking absently out of the window towards the mountains, his weather-beaten old face expressionless.

Heidi immediately started cleaning and straightening up the Alm-hut. She was here, there and everywhere with her duster and mop, and when the dusting met with her satisfaction, she started to polish the glass and pewter vigorously.

Grandfather looked up. "That's enough, Heidi. Enough!"

"But I want to leave everything clean," said Heidi softly.

"Enough. I said enough," barked the old man.

Obediently, Heidi put the pewter back on the shelf and returned the mop, duster and cloths to the cupboard. She then brought a little wicker basket to the table and started to collect and pack her few belongings.

The packing seemed to disturb Grandfather even more, and in an attempt to ease the strain of the situation he spoke almost soothingly.

"Luzern's a fine place. The cousins are good people," he said.

"But you told me they didn't want me to live with them—that is, before, when my mother died." Heidi continued her packing as she spoke.

"They've changed. You've changed."

Heidi did not respond, but, with a determined look, folded up the dress that her grandfather had brought back from Dörfli for her last birthday.

Grandfather stopped rocking and rose abruptly to his feet. "Heidi," he almost shouted. His tone was partly a plea and partly a call for attention. Still standing, he continued more quietly. "You're so young—I'm so old. This'll be best for everyone."

Heidi nodded, though unconvinced.

Grandfather sank into his rocker and, leaning his head back, closed his eyes. Heidi brought a rug that was on her stool and, unfolding it, wrapped it gently over the old man's lap and legs. She then closed the wicker basket carefully and slowly climbed up the wooden ladder to the loft, taking the basket with her. Halfway up the ladder she looked down at the figure in the rocking chair and, assuring herself that the old man was dozing peacefully, continued up to her room.

All was now quiet in the Alm-hut. A single oil lamp dimly lit the stube, casting dark shadows against the yellow light on the rough walls. Through the windows the moon silhouetted the sharp peaks of the mountains. The night was deepening. Heidi knelt beside her bed, her lips moving silently. After a few moments, she got up and slipped between the covers.

"Good night, Grandfather." Her words broke the silence of the night. Down below the old man stirred.

"Good night, Heidi."

He sat up and looked toward the loft, then slowly rose and shuffled to the foot of the ladder. He had a tremendous compulsion to go to her and tell her the truth, to comfort her and be comforted. His powerful hands gripped the ladder. But then he hesitated and, moving to the table, turned off the lamp and lay back once more in his chair. All was still again within the hut. Outside, the fir trees murmured in the gentle wind.

The next morning, when day broke, threatening clouds were scurrying from the west. But Grandfather, with all the wisdom of the mountain folk, had already decided that, with the increasing wind, there would be no rain before nightfall. Heidi, with one last look around the shed and carrying her basket of possessions, joined her grandfather on the downward path toward Dörfli.

Not a word was said till they neared the farm of Peter's parents. It was a neat little farmhouse, yet larger and more prosperous looking than the Alm-hut. Jacob and Brigitte Lange, Peter's father and mother, had great hopes that one day their only son would take over the farm and become as respected and hardworking as his father. But there was time enough for that, and now they only wanted Peter to work at his lessons in school and during the summer holidays enjoy the healthy air of the mountains with his friend Heidi.

The Langes, with Peter, were standing at the farm gate when Heidi and her grandfather arrived. "Grützis" were exchanged and Heidi looked at Peter and seemed about to say something when Jacob Lange patted the Alm-Uncle on the shoulder.

"We'll walk down to the bus stop with you," he said.

"If you like—" replied the old man absently.

Brigitte Lange broke in, "Heidi's one of the family. We'll go as far with her as we can." She clasped Heidi in a motherly hug, smiling down at her. Peter, at the same time, reached for Heidi's basket.

"I'll carry it," he said, as if asserting his male protectiveness.

"It isn't heavy," smiled Heidi, still holding the basket firmly.

"Don't be so stubborn, Heidi."

At that, Heidi released her hold of the basket

and the group started down the path to Dörfli.

Peter and Heidi moved ahead of the others. They walked in silence for a few moments, then Peter said slowly, "Maybe you'll come back sometimes—to see your grandfather." There was another pause.

"Grandfather won't be here. I hope I can visit him in Chur."

Peter glanced back nervously at the three grown-ups who were following. He lowered his voice, as if about to confide an important secret.

"He's not going to Chur. Last night I heard Mama and Father talking. There's no job for your grandfather in Chur, or anywhere else."

Heidi looked at him sharply, with uncomprehending surprise. "Then why is he sending me away?"

"He thinks he's going blind," said Peter seriously. Heidi grabbed Peter by the arm and stopped in the middle of the path. Peter regretted that he'd said anything.

"I shouldn't have told you," he shyly admitted.

"Put down my basket," ordered Heidi. Uncertainly, Peter obeyed. Now how was he going to explain this to the others, who by now had caught up with them.

"What's going on?" asked the Alm-Uncle. Heidi moved off the path to a large boulder, plumped herself down on it and crossed her arms in a defiant gesture.

"Why did you lie to me, Grandfather?" she

asked in a firm voice. The old man was visibly startled and taken aback.

"That's no question for a child to ask her grandfather."

"Between you and me—the truth always. Isn't that what you said?" Heidi persisted. Grandfather was at a loss for an answer.

Brigitte, sensing a family crisis developing, tactfully and soothingly suggested, "We'll wait for you farther down. Come on, Peterli." She took the reluctant Peter's arm and urged him down the slope. Jacob Lange followed, but not before he'd searched Grandfather's face, trying to decide the outcome of this sudden change in events. Heidi was now earnestly addressing her grandfather.

"You knew if you told me the truth I'd never leave you." Grandfather, seemingly ignoring her, said firmly, "You have to go."

Heidi settled herself even more solidly on the boulder. Grandfather continued, "You need grown-ups to take care of you. Stay here and you'll end up taking care of me."

Heidi was not to be dissuaded.

"We'll take care of each other," she said softly, but with a positive air of determination.

The old man sat down beside her on the boulder. "You don't know what it'll be like—" he said gently, looking down at her. Heidi became practical.

"Have you been to a doctor?"

Grandfather shook his head.

"Well, that's what we'll do first," Heidi continued. "A doctor will know how to help you."

"I'm old and my eyes are worn out," the old man said slowly. "No doctor can change that. I'm sorry I lied to you. That was wrong. But sending you to Luzern is right."

"I've always tried to do what you told me," said Heidi. "But if you tell me to leave you when you need me, I won't do it."

But Grandfather would not give in.

"If I decide to put you on that bus, I'll put you on that bus."

Heidi retorted, "I'll come back."

They looked at each other for a moment, and then the old man shook his head. He realized he was weakening in his determination to carry through his plan, and he didn't know whether to laugh or cry. He was between joy and sadness and could not decide which was uppermost. He spoke almost to himself, at the same time addressing the meadows and the mountains.

"What did I do?" he asked. "Somebody tell me what I did to deserve this stubborn, disobedient, disrespectful child?" He paused. "All right. We'll try it." With that, the old man pulled Heidi into his arms in a bear hug. They both climbed down from the boulder and returned to the path. As they waved to the Langes below them, Grandfather pointed towards the Alm-hut high up the mountain. Heidi picked up her basket and, taking Grandfather's hand, set off with him up the trail they had so sadly taken only a few hours before.

But now they were both smiling, and Heidi was happily chattering as the two disappeared into the distance towards the hut. The black clouds, which earlier had warned of possible bad weather, had now vanished, and the sun was shining on the Falknis. This change in the sky confirmed the Alm-Uncle's weather forecast. Or perhaps it was a good omen. But as all mountain people know, the weather can change rapidly and dark clouds can appear again as quickly as they blew away.

Chapter IV
THE RUNAWAY

The postbus left Dörfli twice a day for Maienfeld. From there it made a circular route through other villages to Bad Ragaz before returning to Dörfli several hours later. The main purpose of this little bus was to deliver and collect mail, and it was maintained by the Swiss Postal Service. But it also carried passengers. The postbus was used by the villagers of Dörfli to visit neighboring towns and villages and was a common sight chugging its way down the narrow road to Maienfeld, its usual route being restricted to the autobahn from Sargans to Chur, then on to the southern mountain resorts of Arosa, Davos or St. Moritz.

So, on this September afternoon a few weeks after school had started, the arrival of a large blue bus with lettering on the side "NORDSTROM SCHOOL FOR GIRLS—ZURICH" caused no little attention as it pulled up outside the Alpenrose. People popped their heads out of windows on the main street, and those sitting on the terrace of the gasthaus enjoying a beer and the early autumn sunshine turned their heads to see who was visiting

the village. The owner of the Alpenrose appeared
at the door wiping his hands on his apron in antici-
pation of an increased afternoon beer trade. He
quickly looked round the terrace counting the
number of empty chairs. But he was soon disap-
pointed. When the bus driver opened the door, out
stepped an attractive but obviously agitated lady
in her mid-thirties, followed by an excited group
of about twenty chattering schoolgirls. The worried and weary lady, whom the girls addressed as
Madame Agnes, was doing her best to count her
charges as they poured off the bus and formed a
scattered group outside the Alpenrose. The girls
all seemed to be talking at once, and the drinkers
at the gasthaus treated the whole scene with great
interest.

Madame Agnes raised her voice over the noisy
crowd of girls. "Mesdemoiselles! Young ladies!
Please! If you must chatter so loudly, use French!
It's less strident!"

Madame Agnes raised her hands and, in mock
protest, covered her ears. At that moment, a
plumpish girl broke away from the group and
headed for the Alpenrose entrance.

"Kari—wait. We'll all go in together."

"But I'm starving," protested Kari, who looked
far from underfed.

"Only tea and cakes here," ordered Madame
Agnes in French. "We'll have a nice dinner in
Luzern."

Having herded her noisy flock into the gasthaus,
Madame Agnes, counting rapidly on her fingers,

realized one of her girls was missing. The land-lord meantime, rubbing his hands and bowing, was doing his best to seat his new-found customers, some on the terrace and others around the tables in the stube. Madame Agnes returned to the bus. On the back seat, an attractive girl of about ten, her dark hair fashionably shaped, was sitting staring out of the bus window. She seemed withdrawn and unhappy and was nervously twisting and un-twisting her fingers.

"Come along, Elizabeth," encouraged Madame Agnes, with false brightness in her voice.

Elizabeth's reply was sullen.

"I don't want any tea."

"At least you can stretch your legs."

Madame Agnes had long ago become resigned to Elizabeth's attitude which was strange and aloof, compared to her other girls. And, goodness knows, the others weren't always easy.

"I'll wait here," said Elizabeth.

"Very well." Madame Agnes gave up the struggle and climbed down off the bus.

Elizabeth continued to stare moodily out of the window when something caught her attention, and she pressed her nose against the glass. School was out, and children in twos and threes were happily playing and dancing down the street. Heidi and Peter had started a game of "Follow the Leader," and Peter was leading the children, hopping on one leg. Heidi and the others followed, some tottering, some half-tumbling, but all laughing merrily as they tried to follow Peter's antics.

Elizabeth was fascinated. Why, in this little village the children seemed so happy and full of life.

In Peter's path as he hopped down the street lay a huge dog, fast asleep. He could be a St. Bernard, thought Elizabeth, but she couldn't see the dog's face clearly. Peter took a giant hop over the sleeping dog, and as Heidi and the others followed, the animal stirred and tried to raise its head. Just as the last little boy tried to hop over him, the dog rose, stretching his legs, and the child found himself astride the dog's back. Like a Shetland pony, thought Elizabeth, smiling.

The schoolchildren had stopped their game and gathered round the large dog, clapping their hands and jumping up and down in glee. Peter gently lifted the little boy off the dog's back and looked at Heidi, laughing.

The children, leaving the dog to resume his sleep, all moved in a happy band towards the Alpenrose. They examined the strange bus carefully and Peter, seeing the dirt and mud on the coach body, drew the initial "P" with his finger on the dusty surface. The others followed his example, and soon the side of the bus was covered with letters of various sizes. Heidi was the last, and just as she was drawing a large "H" a movement at the bus window caught her eye and, looking up, she saw Elizabeth. The two girls stared at each other for a moment as their eyes met. Heidi smiled and waved, but Elizabeth seemed to hesitate in acknowledging the friendly greeting. Peter called

Heidi to follow him, and Heidi, turning from the
bus, ran after Peter. It was then that Elizabeth
waved, but Heidi had joined the others and was
unaware that her greeting had been returned.

For a few moments, Elizabeth continued to look
out of the window. Then she stood up, straightened her uniform and stepped down from the bus.
In the distance, down the street, the Dörfli schoolchildren were exchanging "wiedersehn's" and going their separate ways home. Elizabeth, watching
them, saw the girl who had waved at her turn off
the main street and disappear up an alley with
the boy she recognized as the leader of the game.

Heidi and Peter soon left the chalets on the
outskirts of the village and started on the trail that
led to the Alm-hut far up the mountain. Elizabeth followed the main street to the alley and
stood there hesitating as she watched the figures
of the boy and girl grow smaller as they climbed
up the Alpine meadows. When they were almost
out of sight, Elizabeth seemed to make her mind
up and, after a quick look back at the Alpenrose,
hurried down the alley and towards the mountain
path.

In the distance she heard the persistent blasts
of the bus horn, but she ignored the summoning
calls and, with greater determination, strode up
the path, soon leaving the village, just a cluster of
rooftops below.

In the meantime, outside the Alpenrose, Hans
Baumes in his capacity as "polizist" was doing his
best to pacify Madame Agnes. This was made

somewhat difficult by the shrill chatter of the Nordstrom schoolgirls, who were clustered round the bus and were shouting their own suggestions in an effort to solve the problem that was obviously developing between the police official and their governess.

"I'm sorry, Madame," said Hans Baumes in his most official matter-of-fact tone, "but nobody seems to have noticed your missing girl. Perhaps," he added hopefully, "she's wandered off to play with some of our youngsters."

"That isn't like Elizabeth."

"Well, Madame, we'll make a house-to-house search," assured Hans Baumes.

"It's absolutely imperative that we reach Luzern not one second later than seven o'clock, or our entire schedule will be ruined," said Madame Agnes. "Officer, suppose I leave some money with you. When Elizabeth turns up, which I'm sure she will when it gets dark, perhaps you would phone the school."

Madame Agnes took a card and some money from her handbag.

"Here's the phone number. If you could see she has proper lodging for the night, I'll arrange that tomorrow one of her teachers or her father picks her up." As Madame Agnes emphasized her words "proper lodging," she had glanced down the street at the quaint old houses with their weathered crossbeams and bright geranium window boxes until she saw a wrought iron sign on the Alpenrose wall. Madame Agnes sniffed. She supposed this gasthaus would have to do and only hoped Elizabeth's father, Herr Wyler, would approve.

Hans was not too happy about Madame Agnes's request nor too sure about the correctness in accepting the money. But he put the new twenty franc note in his pocket.

"Won't she feel upset, being left in a strange place?" he asked.

"This isn't the first time, and it won't be the last. I'm sure I can rely on you."

Hans straightened his back proudly at this vote of confidence. Twenty francs, after all, represented the profit on two pairs of shoes, and although he was fairly well off, he could hardly reject a little extra beer money just for doing his duty.

"All right—I'll do my best." Hans wasn't too certain exactly what he was going to do, but one lost little girl in a small village could present no great problem. He'd handled more difficult situations than that in the past. But this was different. Hans looked down the street again, hoping that he'd spot Elizabeth before the bus left. But then he'd have to give back the twenty francs. That would be the only decent thing to do, he mused. His thoughts were interrupted by Madame Agnes, who was now loading her passengers on the bus.

"Thank you, officer," she said to Hans Baumes. Then, directing her attention to her girls, she called out, "Everyone board; on the bus, everyone. Quickly. *Allons, allons, mes enfants.*"

The bus door slammed shut; the engine roared into life, and a few moments later, the bus disappeared in a cloud of dust on the little winding road to Maienfeld.

After nearly an hour's climb, Heidi and Peter reached his parents' farm. Swinging his books off his back, Peter shook hands and, with a quick "Wiedersehn," went into the farmhouse as Heidi resumed her journey to the Alm-hut alone. Unknown to either of them, and still out of sight on the path below the Langes' farmhouse, the now-weary Elizabeth continued her upward trek in search of Heidi.

When Heidi reached the porch of the Alm-hut twilight was already falling. Grandfather, hearing her steps, opened the door to greet her.

"I was going to start down to meet you," he said.

"I'm no later than usual, Grandfather."

"But it seems so dark." The old man looked at Heidi lovingly and then down towards the Rhine valley. With an absent expression, Grandfather ran his hand across his eyes. Heidi watched him, her face clouding with concern. In the background, from the direction of the shed, came the rising clamor of the goats and chickens. The two went inside the hut and Heidi closed the door.

"How did you get along today, Grandfather?"

"Fine," he replied as Heidi lit the oil lamp.

"I don't like to leave you here all by yourself," she said, busily tidying the table. The clamor from the animals outside increased.

"Now what's set off those goats and chickens?" queried Grandfather, peering out of the window.

Seeing nothing, he opened the door and went out, followed by Heidi, who was even more anxious to discover the cause of the uproar in the shed.

The old man tramped towards the shed and, as he did so, Elizabeth, who had reached the Alm-hut while they were both inside, darted from behind the shed to the corner of the hut. But neither Heidi nor her grandfather saw any movement in the darkening evening shadows.

Grandfather continued towards the shed, with its clamor of goat calls and frantic clucking of the chickens, while Heidi moved around to the opposite corner of the hut, both looking for the cause of the commotion. By this time, Elizabeth had almost circled the Alm-hut, looking again for the trail, so that she might escape down the mountain and into the night. In the dark she had glimpsed the figure of the Alm-Uncle, who had looked enormous and frightening, and to Elizabeth, in her search for Heidi, a most unexpected and terrifying apparition. Despite her fatigue, she ran round the hut and, as she reached the far corner, ran full tilt into Heidi. Both girls fell to the ground with yells of mixed surprise and fear. Grandfather, hearing the shouts, hurried over, just as Heidi and Elizabeth were scrambling to their feet. He looked first at Heidi.

"Are you all right?"

"I think so, Grandfather." Heidi was as surprised as anyone at this encounter. The old man gripped Elizabeth's arm, his hand shaking.

"And where did you come from?" he asked. "Let's have a better look at you—inside."

Elizabeth struggled for a moment.

Grandfather, still holding Elizabeth by the arm, steered her towards the door of the hut. Heidi followed them.

Chapter V
THE VISITOR

Once inside the hut, Heidi turned up the oil lamp and as she saw Elizabeth more clearly immediately recognized her.

"Why, you're the girl on the bus!"

The three were standing in the center of the room. Heidi turned from Elizabeth to her grandfather.

"She was sitting by herself in a bus in Dörfli."

This explanation puzzled the old man who, turning to Elizabeth, asked, "Why did you follow Heidi up here?"

At this, Elizabeth retreated to the table and slumped down on Heidi's little chair. Although almost overcome with fatigue, she was determined to explain her presence here to the old man. She answered slowly, with sullen defiance.

"I was bored. It was something to do." And then, almost to herself, she whispered, "Heidi. I like that name."

Heidi sat down opposite her in Grandfather's larger chair. With her elbows on the table and hands clasped, Heidi leaned towards Elizabeth with a friendly smile. "What's your name?"

"Elizabeth. Some day I'm going to have it changed."

Grandfather sank into his rocker, seeming more relaxed. He studied the two girls and, lighting his pipe, carefully asked, "So now you're here, what are we going to do with you?"

"I'll go back to the village. Sooner or later they'll send someone after me," sighed Elizabeth.

Grandfather puffed at his pipe. "You can't go down the mountain by yourself in the dark. I'll take you in the morning."

Elizabeth looked at the old man inquiringly.

"Where do I stay till morning?"

Grandfather tapped his pipe against the fireplace. He was now rather enjoying the situation.

"Well, the goats are friendly. They'll make room for you in the shed." He chuckled to himself. Heidi looked at the old man reprovingly.

"Grandfather—"

"Oh, we'll work out something. Now—let's wash up, get the table set and have our supper. I get impatient at runaway girls when my stomach's empty."

Heidi smiled with relief, happy that her grandfather had accepted her new friend, at least for the time being. Jumping down from the table, Heidi led Elizabeth to the pitcher and basin and found her a clean towel from the closet. Then she busied herself with preparing the simple meal of bread, cheese and goat's milk. Elizabeth hovered around her, every now and then giving a helping hand.

Soon the three were sitting down to their meal. Grandfather had moved his rocker to the table, and Heidi now insisted Elizabeth take the larger chair, while she sat in her usual place.

"You say grace, Grandfather," said Heidi. The short prayer over, the three began their meal.

Heidi filled the glasses with sweet goat's milk and passed the thick slices of homemade bread. They all ate silently and contentedly, and it was as if this scene had been repeated every night. The old man, munching his bread and cheese in his rocker, and the two little girls sitting opposite each other, happily drinking their milk. The oil lamp shone brightly and the logs in the fireplace crackled, giving a friendly glow. The Alm-hut was at peace with the world.

Though Heidi and her grandfather had finished their meal, Elizabeth was still eating the last piece of bread enthusiastically.

"Mine wasn't the only empty stomach," said Grandfather, pushing his rocker back from the table.

Elizabeth exclaimed, "I never tasted food like this."

Grandfather relit his pipe. "Very simple," he said between puffs, "which nowadays makes it hard to find. People complicate everything, even honest bread and cheese."

Elizabeth looked around the Alm-hut, taking

in every detail of the cozy room. "You know, I can't believe this place. No electricity, no running water, no car and no television."

"We don't need those things," said Grandfather softly and kindly.

"In Peter's house they have electricity," said Heidi, "and a big radio. And I saw television the day Grandfather took me to Bad Ragaz."

Elizabeth was still looking around the room. "I like it this way."

"Where do you live?" asked Heidi.

The smile faded from Elizabeth's face. "The school's in Zurich."

Grandfather turned to Elizabeth. "But what about your family?"

Elizabeth dropped her head. "I don't have a family, well—apart from my father. His offices are in Zurich, but he travels all the time. He's very famous."

"I'm sure your friends on the bus are wondering where you are," said Heidi, changing the subject.

"They're not my friends," responded Elizabeth quickly. "I haven't got time for friends."

Heidi raised her eyebrows. Time was never a problem for her. Provided she got to school before the bell stopped ringing and fed the animals and looked after her grandfather, she had all the time she wanted. And friends, why they were one of the most important things in life. Heidi was puzzled.

Grandfather broke the pause by asking, "What does your father do to make him so famous?"

"He's the head of Wyler-Dietrich, the best hotel training school there is. All the great hotels are run by people my father trained." Elizabeth paused and then with a touch of bitterness quoted, "The men who make millions feel at home—wherever they are in the world."

Neither Heidi nor her grandfather knew what to say. They all sat quietly. The old man puffed his pipe, his bushy eyebrows twitching. Elizabeth turned towards the window, listening to the night. The wind was whistling in the firs.

Later that evening, high in the loft, Heidi and Elizabeth lay side by side in the big bed. Moonlight shone on the old wooden beams, and through the skylight they could see dark clouds racing across the stars. For some minutes, they had been together in silence, then Heidi spoke quietly.

"Elizabeth doesn't seem the right name for you."

"Heidi's perfect for you." Elizabeth was drowsy, but in her half-sleep heard Heidi whisper.

"Has anybody ever called you Bet?"

"No."

"It suits you."

"Bet—Bet," repeated Elizabeth slowly.

"Can I call you that?"

"If you want to."

I'd really like to call her "Betli," Heidi thought. But "Little Bet" wouldn't be too polite for anyone my age, considering she is as big as I am.

Elizabeth was more awake now and raised herself on one elbow, turning towards Heidi.

"Why do you live with your grandfather?"

"My mother and father died."

"I'm sorry. Do you remember them?" asked Elizabeth.

"Mama, just a little. At least I think I do. When Grandfather tells stories, I can see her, almost hear her." Heidi paused. "You said you lived with your father?"

"I don't really live with him"—Elizabeth emphasized the 'with'—"since my mother died."

"Do you remember her?"

There was a note of sadness in Elizabeth's reply.

"Oh, yes. I remember her. I feel closer to mother than anybody."

"And your father?" asked Heidi.

"All he cares about is work. Oh, we used to have fun—you know, special jokes and games—in the old days. But, since mother's gone he doesn't seem to want to be near me. When we have to be together, he's either sad or angry. He's gone farther away than mother—" Her voice trailed off and she hoped Heidi could not see the tears welling in her eyes. Heidi, sensing her sorrow, put an arm around Elizabeth's shoulders.

"Bet," she said softly,

"Umm?"

"You said you didn't have time for friends."

"That's right," agreed Elizabeth.

"I was hoping you might have time for just one."

"I think I might."

Moonbeams splintered the dark shadows of the loft. Two little girls smiled at each other, then fell into a deep sleep, filled with dreams of the future.

Chapter VI
THE PHONE CALL

The next morning, after letting the children sleep late, Grandfather took them down the mountain path to Dörfli. Elizabeth was much brighter than the night before. Every so often the children ran from the path to pick autumn crocus, then, rejoining Grandfather, each grasped one of his gnarled old hands and skipped down the Alpine meadow trail. Between them Grandfather proudly stomped his carved stick into the ground at every step.

They reached the Alpenrose before the sun was at its height and entered the lobby.

Grandfather, who still treated the telephone as an invention of the devil, persuaded the gasthaus waitress to place the call to Zurich. When the number was ringing, Elizabeth took over the receiver.

"May I speak with Herr Wyler, please. This is his daughter."

The woman's voice at the other end was efficient and businesslike.

"Herr Wyler's office."

"Mady—it's me," said Elizabeth, recognizing the voice as belonging to her father's secretary.

"Elizabeth! You promised you wouldn't run away again!"

"May I speak with my father?" Elizabeth said firmly.

"He's in conference most of the day. We'll be coming to pick you up tomorrow."

Elizabeth imagined Mady had already made a note of this in her appointment book.

"Tomorrow?" she questioned.

"Yes—I've already spoken to the police officer there. Does he know you're all right?"

"Yes."

Elizabeth shifted from one foot to the other, feeling the increasing pressure of authority at the other end of the phone.

"Where are you now?" asked Mady.

"At the gasthaus—the Alpenrose."

"We'll meet you there at noon tomorrow. Would you like me to speak to the proprietor?"

"No. I'm fine." Elizabeth was becoming resigned to these reunions. History was repeating itself.

"Please, Elizabeth, try and stay out of mischief till tomorrow. We'll see you then. Wiedersehn."

"Wiedersehn," said Elizabeth, then, with a quick look at the receiver, slammed it down on the phone.

Heidi and her grandfather waited expectantly for Elizabeth's report, although from her replies, they had both understood the general conversation.

"My father's coming for me tomorrow."

Grandfather tried to appear as matter of fact in his tone as possible.

"So we'll arrange for you to have a room here."

"Please, Grandfather," pleaded Heidi, taking the old man's hand, "can't Bet stay with us. She can come to school with me, help me with the chores and . . ."

"I promise not to do anything to make you cross —Grandfather!" interrupted Elizabeth imploringly.

Grandfather, smiling, looked down at the two girls.

"All right—off with you," he said.

Heidi and Elizabeth pushed open the Alpenrose door and happily ran up the street hand in hand.

Grandfather, still smiling, looked round the gasthaus stube and, seeing no familiar face, slowly followed the girls into the midday sunshine.

On their return to the Alm-hut later that day, Elizabeth insisted she help Heidi with her housework, and when this was completed, they both went to the shed to tend to the animals. On the climb up the mountain, Heidi told her new friend all about her summer holidays, how she and Peter took the goats to the upper slopes, told her about the mountains in winter and spring and described so much of her life with her grandfather that Elizabeth felt she had known Heidi forever. Elizabeth had already met Peter, and on their return journey, they had all stopped at the farmhouse to chat with Peter's parents and enjoy a cool glass of lemonade. Although she had only arrived at Dörfli yesterday, Elizabeth already felt at home on the mountain and with its people and had discovered a way of life here that was new and refreshing. Such was Heidi's enthusiasm and genuine love for the countryside that, listening to her stories and descriptions of the Alm, Elizabeth realized that Zurich and the big city way of living was not all the world had to offer. Up here at the Alm-hut, as she felt the cool mountain breezes on her face and looked down at the valley of the Rhine far below, the city and her school seemed a thousand kilometers away.

In the shed Heidi introduced Elizabeth to all the animals by name as she fed the chickens and refilled the water pails for the goats. Elizabeth met Bärli and Schwänli and listened, fascinated, as Heidi described all the different personalities of Schnecke, Schneehöpli, Distelfinck and Big Turk.

At the moment, Elizabeth was trying to get better acquainted with Bärli, though the two of them were eyeing each other with no little distrust.

Heidi stroked Bärli's neck, putting her face against his soft coat.

"He won't hurt you—he wants to be friendly," Heidi encouraged her. Elizabeth hesitated, raising her hand. She was trying to get up enough courage to stroke the animal. Bärli couldn't decide whether Elizabeth was going to pet or strike him, so he stood his ground, glaring at her.

"There's nothing to be afraid of," said Heidi.

With an effort, Elizabeth stroked Bärli's head, and as she did so, all her fears and suspicions vanished. She petted him more enthusiastically and at last even rested her head against his neck. Bärli responded by licking Elizabeth's hand.

"See how easy it is, you two, when you trust each other," cried Heidi with delight.

Elizabeth nodded, smiling.

Later that night, after the moon had risen, Elizabeth and Heidi were again side by side in the comfortable loft bed. It was dark and still, but sleep seemed far away for both little girls. There were tears on Elizabeth's cheeks.

"Bet," whispered Heidi.

"I thought you were asleep."

"We can talk if you want to."

"Grandfather will be cross," said Elizabeth, sniffing.

"Not if we whisper."

"There's nothing to talk about." Elizabeth choked back a sob. Heidi reached across the bed, touching the tears on Elizabeth's cheek.

"Oh, Bet—don't cry."

"But I keep thinking about tomorrow; it's the end of everything."

"We're friends, aren't we?" Heidi said gently.

There was no answer.

"Bet?"

"Yes."

"So it isn't the end. It's just the beginning." Heidi's words were soft and gentle. Just then, below in the stube, Grandfather cleared his throat noisily. Both girls froze. His voice seemed to shatter the still of the night.

"Heidi—Bet! I know you're both too respectful to disobey me by staying awake, but your talking in your sleep is keeping me awake!"

Then all was quiet. The girls, with a giggle, settled down to sleep. A bird called in the night, and the fir trees murmured their answer.

Chapter VII
THE RUNAWAY RETURNS

The next day, outside the Alpenrose, a group of small boys were clustered round a large shining sports car. They walked around the car in wonder, some suggesting it must be a rare Italian make, others that it had to have cost a fortune. Hans Baumes, in his official capacity, was keeping an eye on the car and the admiring youngsters.

"Keep your hands off it," he shouted. Then, seeing the Alm-Uncle approaching, followed by Heidi, Elizabeth and Peter, he moved away from the car and greeted them.

"Grützi, Wilhelm. Grützi, Heidi, Grützi, Grützi."

"Grützi, Hans."

"That's my father's car," exclaimed Elizabeth. Peter's eyes opened wide.

"My goodness, that looks like something out of the Grand Prix," and he ran to join the admiring crowd.

Hans spoke to the Alm-Uncle.

"Herr Wyler is waiting inside, Wilhelm," he said, waving his hand toward the gasthaus.

"Thank you," said Grandfather, leading Heidi and Elizabeth to the door of the Alpenrose.

Daniel Wyler was sitting at a table in the far corner of the gasthaus stube, an open briefcase beside him. Mady, who had just finished taking dictation, was gathering up papers scattered over the table.

Dan Wyler looked up as Grandfather and the girls entered. He was a good-looking man in his mid-thirties, and his general appearance, from his well-tailored suit to his air of self-assurance, denoted success.

He was indeed successful in his business life. It was only his relationship with his daughter that worried him, and he was perhaps not aware that it worried Elizabeth even more.

Dan Wyler and Mady rose to their feet. Her father gave Elizabeth a quick embrace, pecking her on the cheek.

"Elizabeth—what are we going to do with you?" asked Dan Wyler, surveying the child and frowning.

Mady stepped quickly forward and gave Elizabeth a warm hug.

"She actually looks better for her experience," she exclaimed brightly. Dan Wyler turned to Grandfather and Heidi and introduced himself. They shook hands.

"I'm Wilhelm Beck and this is my granddaughter, Heidi," said Grandfather stiffly. Dan Wyler looked at Mady.

"This is my secretary, Fräulein Roush. How can

I thank you properly for taking care of my runaway?"

"She was no trouble," replied Grandfather.

"Bet helped with the work," exclaimed Heidi
brightly.

Dan Wyler gave Elizabeth a surprised look.

"Bet? Is that the name you gave them?"

Heidi spoke up quickly. "No, sir—it's the name
I gave her."

"I see," said Dan Wyler slowly, taking out his
wallet. "Well, I'm very grateful and I'd like to
show my appreciation."

At this Grandfather straightened his back and
waved away the offered money.

"Bet was a guest," he said deliberately. Then,
looking down at Elizabeth with a smile, he added
warmly, "She'll always be welcome."

"That's very generous of you, Herr Beck." Dan
Wyler grasped his briefcase. "Well, Elizabeth," he
said in his businesslike voice, "it's a long drive back
to Zurich."

Elizabeth dropped her head.

"I'm not going back."

Mady interrupted, trying to ease the difficult situation. "The school's agreed to take you—on pro-
bation."

But Elizabeth was defiant. "I'm not going with
you. I'm staying with Heidi."

"But you know that's impossible," said her
father.

"Then let Heidi come with us," suggested Elizabeth.

Heidi, realizing that Dan Wyler, as a parent, wielded the authority, appealed to Elizabeth.

"Bet—we can write to each other."

"That isn't the same."

"Elizabeth, be reasonable." Dan Wyler was becoming impatient at the delay. Heidi, in an effort to help her friend, took Elizabeth's hand.

"Maybe Grandfather and I can come and visit you."

"Yes. We might do that," Grandfather added rather uncertainly. With his present problems still on his mind, he could not foresee a trip to Zurich in his future.

Dan Wyler, sensing a feeling of cooperation from Elizabeth's new friends, quickly interjected, "And some day maybe you can come back and see Heidi."

"Do you promise?" asked Elizabeth, looking up at her father.

"Yes, yes. Now come along." Dan Wyler was thinking that he'd already wasted nearly a whole business day. Mady collected her papers, and the party moved towards the door. Outside, Peter was waiting for them.

"Wiedersehn, Bet," said Peter, holding out his hand. Elizabeth shook his hand warmly.

"Wiedersehn, Peter."

"Come back soon," said Grandfather, giving Elizabeth a quick hug. Heidi and Elizabeth sadly embraced without a word. Dan Wyler opened the car door.

"Once again—vielen dank—many thanks." He got

behind the wheel. Elizabeth sat stiffly between her father and Mady. The car started and moved quickly away. Heidi, Peter and Grandfather waved, but Elizabeth did not respond, looking straight ahead. She did not want them to see the tears streaming down her cheeks. The car got smaller, then vanished round a bend. The old man and the children stood silently outside the gasthaus, still looking down the road. All they could see now was a dwindling cloud of dust.

Chapter VIII
THE LETTER

Some weeks later Grandfather was chopping wood outside the Alm-hut. The afternoon was cool and the old man had wrapped a scarf around his neck for warmth. He paused, sniffing the autumn air. There was no mistaking the season. The smell of the leaves and the grass and the increasing winds all told of winter that was not far away. He must build up a good supply of logs. Every now and then he picked up an armful and carefully stacked it in neat rows on the woodpile. Soon the snow would come and work would be more difficult.

Inside the hut, Heidi was sitting in her own chair at the table, writing. She was using a school notebook for writing paper, and she bit into the pencil in thought. Heidi was writing in German, as she was taught in school and which they sometimes referred to as "High German." Everyone in the district, and in fact in almost all German-speaking Switzerland, used Schweitzer-deutsch or "Swiss-German," which was a spoken dialect and not a language to be written. Pausing in her work, she picked up an opened letter lying on the table.

Although her grandfather had only brought it yesterday from the post office, Heidi must have read it a dozen times, now knowing its contents by heart. She read it once more, then resumed her writing, slowly repeating her words as she wrote.

> *I read your letter to Peter and Grandfather, and we all laughed when you told us about the clown at the Zurich circus. Now Peter wants to be a clown.*

Smiling to herself, Heidi gazed out of the window at the scurrying clouds. A few moments later she again picked up Elizabeth's letter and read—

> *My father was in Cairo for two weeks, training the staff of a new hotel. I ran away again, but this time I didn't meet any nice people. I think of you and Peter and Grandfather all the time. I think of Bärli, too, and miss you all. Your friend—Bet.*

Two little kisses were at the bottom of the page, and Heidi felt a wave of sadness. But she was happy to receive Elizabeth's letter. Putting the letter in the envelope, and once again looking at the address and the colorful postage stamp, Heidi returned to her notebook.

> *We're sorry you ran away again. I'm going to ask Grandfather if we can visit you after Christmas. But please don't count on it, be-*

cause he's not feeling well and I'm trying to get him to see a doctor. All of your friends in Dörfli miss you, especially Heidi.

Then, after adding a little cross after her name, Heidi carefully removed the page from the notebook, folded it and addressed the envelope. She would take the letter to the post office tomorrow on the way to school.

Outside, Grandfather placed the last of the cut logs on the pile. As he straightened his back and stretched, darkness covered his eyes. The Alm-hut and the shed became blurred. He stumbled, and the axe in his hand clattered to the ground just before he fell.

Heidi, who was already at the doorway, ran towards her grandfather, who was lying by the woodpile.

"Grandfather," she cried.

The old man struggled to his feet.

"I tripped. That's all. No damage done."

But Heidi realized that these attacks were becoming more frequent. Holding her grandfather's hand, she spoke as calmly as possible. "Peter's mother says there are lots of good doctors in Bad Ragaz."

"I don't need a doctor to tell me what I know," replied Grandfather gruffly. He wearily picked up the axe. Then they both went into the hut, hand in hand.

Chapter IX
THE SEARCH AND
THE DISAPPEARANCE

The following Sunday Heidi and Peter had promised themselves their last picnic of the year, before the snows fell. Already the white blanket on the peaks had crept lower since summer, but the meadows above the Alm-hut were still green and sprinkled with blue and yellow crocuses. The morning sun broke weakly through the clouds as Heidi packed a basket with bread and cheese and a flask of goat's milk. Then she folded a brightly colored cloth on top and closed the basket lid. Heidi went to the hut door, once more to inspect the weather. She was sure the clouds were clearing. As she was looking towards the mountains, Peter clambered up the last rise to the Alm-hut. Heidi greeted him cheerfully.

"I think the weather will hold," she said.

Peter only grunted and gazed at the sky as he regained his breath. Heidi was keen to start their walk.

"Are you ready?" she called to Peter.

Peter nodded, and the pair set off up the mountain.

When they reached a spot on which they both agreed, Heidi spread out the cloth, smoothing it down carefully over the uneven, coarse grass.

"There's still lots of good pasture. We should have brought the goats."

Peter could not answer immediately, his mouth full of bread and cheese. He munched furiously.

"Sometimes," he said between bites, "sometimes I think you'd rather be with the goats than me."

"Sometimes I would," replied Heidi, scrambling to her feet, "but not mostly."

She looked at the sky where storm clouds were moving in and had already covered the Falknis. The winds were increasing, and Heidi tidied up the cloth and shook it. Crumbs flew into the air and were swept upwards in the windy gusts.

"We should start down," she said.

Peter looked up, screwing his eyes. "There's no snow in those clouds."

Heidi laughed and tapped the brass compass hanging round his neck. "Does your compass give you weather reports, too?"

"You just wish you had a compass," Peter retorted.

"We don't need two," said Heidi.

At that moment, Peter cocked his ear and stared intently towards a clump of bushes a few meters away. Heidi thought he looked like the picture of a bird dog she'd seen in one of her grandfather's books. But she was in no mood for gaiety now, for she sensed something was wrong.

"What is it?" she cried.

"Just go on with what you're doing," answered Peter almost rudely. He made an effort to appear casual, but Peter wasn't a very good actor, thought Heidi. Peter edged towards the clump of bushes, approaching them at an angle.

Heidi instantly recognized the Wild Man, as a long-haired figure leapt from the bushes and sprang in great bounds up the open slopes. Peter dashed after him, putting all his strength into the chase. But the Wild Man was moving at a tremendous speed. For a moment, the strange figure lost his footing and stumbled, sending stones cascading down the slopes. With this momentary advantage, Peter doubled his efforts and seemed to be getting closer. But the Wild Man was on his feet again, zigzagging like a hare as though to confuse his pursuer. They were in open ground now, but Peter knew his quarry was making for the maze of canyons and rocks that lay just beyond the next ridge in the mountain.

"Peter, don't go any farther," Heidi called after him.

Peter heard her cry only faintly, for he had now reached the rocky canyons, and the fugitive had disappeared. Heidi climbed higher till she reached the rise in the open ground and stared in Peter's direction. But she could see nothing. The winds were rising, and standing on the ridge, Heidi was buffeted by the strong gusts. She had difficulty keeping her balance, and was nearly blown off her feet. The wind was becoming angry and great storm clouds darkened the sky.

"Peter—" Heidi called again, but her voice trailed off in the wind and she felt terribly alone. She fought the force of the coming gale as she made her way slowly towards the rocks. But still no sign of Peter or the Wild Man. A rumble of thunder made Heidi look upward towards the Falknis. Black clouds raced across the peaks. Again the thunder rolled threateningly.

"Peter—Peter!" she screamed. But only the mountain heights answered with yet another echo of thunder. Heidi had now crouched down, holding her knees in an effort to withstand the hurricane. A jagged slash of lightning silhouetted the rocks, followed seconds later by a deafening crack of thunder. Heidi decided she must go for help and, getting to her feet unsteadily, turned and battled her way down the slope. Retrieving the picnic basket, she began running as fast as she could. But it was becoming very dark now, and Heidi stumbled along the uneven path. At every new thunder clap she froze and looked back up the mountain. But she could see nothing in the swirling black mist. The rain had started. Single big drops at first, then suddenly a heavy downpour. She could now see the light from the Alm-hut, blurred in the torrential storm. With all her strength she splashed and stumbled towards the hut door, forcing herself to reach shelter. As she approached her grandfather opened the door, and she could see the familiar figure framed in the entrance by the light from the oil lamp. The old man put his arms around her, sheltering her, and swept her into the hut.

"Grandfather," Heidi gasped breathlessly, "Peter—he followed the Wild Man—he didn't come back." Heidi sobbed as she forced out the words. She closed her eyes as if to blot out all thoughts of the storm and Peter's frantic chase. The next few hours were blank in Heidi's memory. Even months later she could not recall whether or not she had slept. All she remembered was sitting in Grandfather's chair wrapped in a blanket and sipping hot chocolate. She must have been asleep, as it was now dark outside, and there was Peter's mother, Brigitte, peering out of the window. Thunder was still rolling and the heavy rain was pounding on the roof.

Heidi looked up at Frau Lange.

"They'll find Peter," she said encouragingly.

"Of course," Frau Lange said calmly.

"He's probably waiting in a cave till the storm's over," said Heidi. Brigitte nodded.

"Like some more chocolate?"

"No, thank you." Heidi put her cup on the table as Brigitte returned to the window. The thunder rattled the panes of glass, and the hurricane whipped the fir trees into a frenzied crescendo.

Later that night, eight dark figures tramped up the mountain from the Alm-hut. They were all wearing thick coats and their heads were covered against the pouring rain. They each carried a lantern or a flashlight, which they waved from side to side slowly, scanning the ground. Thunder was still rolling around the mountains. From the Alm-hut, Heidi could see the flickering specks of light on the heights above, the lanterns like tiny twinkling stars in the distance, bobbing to and fro, appearing then disappearing. The party was led by Grandfather, followed by Peter's father, Jacob Lange, and Hans Baumes. Behind them were five men, willingly recruited from the village by Hans for this midnight search. The five were strung out in a semicircle behind Hans, covering as wide an area as possible.

The Alm-Uncle raised his hand and stopped, the rain lashing his face.

"The storm's washed out any tracks."

"It's hopeless. We'll have to start fresh in the morning," said Hans, grasping the old man's arm. But Jacob Lange was adamant.

"The rest of you go down. I'm not quitting yet."

Grandfather tried to reach a compromise. "Let's give it a little longer," he told Hans. The search party resumed their efforts and trudged slowly up the slope. Each, in his own way, was determined to find the missing boy. Grandfather swung his lantern even more widely, striving to penetrate the stormy dark. Jacob Lange was grimly determined as he shouted his son's name.

"Peter! Peter!" But there was no answer. Only the steady swish of the rain and the roll of the thunder, which now seemed farther away.

"Peterli! Peterli!" called Jacob, even more desperately. During a lull in the thunder, Jacob thought he heard a faint voice in the distance.

"Father—Father."

"Listen!" ordered Jacob Lange. The three men stopped abruptly.

"Father." There was no mistaking it this time. The party turned in the direction of the sound and came upon the large cluster of rocks.

"Father." There it was again and very close. Jacob was the first to see him. Peter was huddled in a rock cleft, blinking as the lantern blinded his eyes. Like a little wet, frightened rabbit, thought Grandfather as he joined Jacob.

Jacob knelt beside the boy and hugged him.

"My ankle," gasped Peter.

Grandfather reached down and gently felt Peter's foot.

"A sprain—I think," he announced.

"It's going to take a while to work our way down," said Jacob.

Hans quickly assumed command.

"We'll go down slowly and stay together."

"We shouldn't waste light. We'll need some in reserve," suggested Grandfather, turning off his lantern. Two of the others followed his example.

"We'll take turns carrying the boy," said Hans. But Jacob, who was holding Peter in his arms, was determined not to let him go.

"I can manage for now."

The party set off slowly, with Hans leading, followed by Jacob. The others straggled behind, with

Grandfather last in line. Hans carried the brightest lantern and every now and then held it up high, guiding his friends down the path, now treacherous with mud. Grandfather, bringing up the rear, leaned heavily on his trusted old stick. The party inched its way down the mountainside, the return journey seeming to be endless. On one side of the path the ground rose sharply, and on the other lay a steep embankment. No one saw Grandfather as he faltered, rubbing the water from his eyes. He strained to see the figure in front of him, but his eyes were blurring. The halo of light from the last lantern was dimming, and then, to his fading eyes, was extinguished. He was now totally sightless, one hand reaching out wildly like a drowning man, the other hand clutching his stick and vainly trying to find the path. His voice lost in the wind, rain and thunder, the old man cried out.

"Wait! Wait! Hans! Jacob! Wait!"

But as the storm raged, his plea for help went unheeded. The party plodded slowly, but steadily, down the slopes, little knowing they had lost their oldest and most gallant companion. Grandfather again stumbled and this time fell, losing his trusted alpenstock in the fall. The old man, groping for his stick, at last managed to struggle to his feet. The rain was driving harder now, and try as he might, the stick could not be found. He dragged his feet a few steps and, losing his balance, with a muffled shriek, plunged over the embankment, headlong into the dark abyss. A sharp flash of lightning made instant daylight on the deserted mountain trail. Then all was black again as angry thunder rolled from distant peaks.

Rain spattered in a large puddle on the path. Across the puddle, forlorn and alone, lay an old carved alpenstock.

Chapter X
THE ALPENSTOCK

It was still dark in the early morning hours when the search party reached the Alm-hut. The wind and the rain had abated slightly. Inside the hut, Heidi was sitting motionless in her grandfather's rocking chair. Brigitte Lange was standing at the window. Seeing the approaching lanterns through sheets of water pouring down the panes, Brigitte called to Heidi.

"They're coming!"

Heidi jumped up from the rocker and joined Brigitte as she opened the door. At the porch there were muttered "Gute nacht's," and Hans led the five volunteers down the path towards Dörfli. Jacob carried Peter into the Alm-hut.

"Only a sprained ankle," said Jacob, setting Peter down gently in the rocker. His mother bent over and gave Peter a hug.

"I'll get you all wet, Mama," protested Peter. Heidi looked up at Jacob Lange.

"Where's Grandfather?" Heidi's voice was steady, with no hint of alarm. Jacob gave Brigitte a quick glance.

"We thought he'd taken one of his shortcuts. That he'd be here ahead of us."

Heidi was shaking her head and then, as if to herself, whispered, "Where could he be?"

Brigitte said soothingly, "Now, Heidi, don't upset yourself. Nobody knows the mountain better than your grandfather."

Jacob put his arm around his wife while looking at Heidi. "My guess is he's taken shelter from this downpour. Soon as the rain eases, he'll be down."

Brigitte added, "You come and spend what's left of the night with us."

Heidi went to the door and peered out into the rain and the dark. She closed the door and stood with her back to it, arms folded and lips pursed.

"No," she said, "I'll wait for Grandfather."

"I'll stay with her. You go along," Brigitte told Jacob, who nodded. Jacob picked up Peter in his arms.

"If your grandfather isn't home by daybreak we'll all go back up the mountain. Get some sleep, Heidi."

Peter, turning his head to Heidi, said, "Tomorrow you can make me a crutch."

"Wiedersehn, Peter."

"Wiedersehn, Heidi."

Jacob, covering Peter's head with his raincoat, opened the door and was enveloped by the night. Brigitte, closing the door behind them, saw Heidi run once more to the window. But Heidi could see nothing but pouring rain. In her mind she could hear her grandfather's voice, which seemed far, far away.

"He's going to be all right," consoled Brigitte.

"I know that," said Heidi. She listened, but all she could hear was the wind lashing the firs.

That night Jacob Lange had little sleep, for he was up and about at daybreak. As soon as he had finished a hurried cup of coffee, he went to his little workshop behind the farmhouse and with his skillful hands made a makeshift crutch for Peter. The crutch completed, he returned to the farmhouse and laid it beside the sleeping boy. Then he went to the kitchen and prepared sandwiches. Hans Baumes would be arriving soon, and together they would climb the mountain in search of the Alm-Uncle. He packed food for both of them in his knapsack and scribbled a short note for Peter, telling his son that he would be back later in the day.

There was a knock on the farmhouse door, and there was Hans, together with two other men from last night's search party. Jacob looked surprised.

"I thought you'd be alone," he said to Hans, though inwardly he was delighted the others were joining them.

"Hans-Uli and Peter the Blacksmith insisted on coming," explained Hans Baumes. The volunteers smiled and nodded to Jacob. "Guten Morgen, Jacob," they said together. Jacob looked at his knapsack.

"Don't worry," said Hans Baumes, patting the

bulging pocket of his coat. "I've brought plenty of food for all of us. Let's get started."

Taking a quick look at the sleeping Peter, Jacob joined the three men on the porch, and the group started up the mountain. This was their second search in only a few hours. They stopped for a moment at the Alm-hut to see if Grandfather had returned.

Brigitte greeted her husband. She whispered, as Heidi was still asleep in the loft.

"No news yet. Good luck!" Brigitte waved as the party climbed up the path towards the upper heights. The rain had stopped, but the skies were still angry, with dark, racing clouds.

Later that afternoon Jacob returned to the Alm-hut. Brigitte and Heidi met him at the porch, and Heidi saw immediately what Jacob was carrying. She grabbed the old carved alpenstock from him, looking at it with wide-open eyes. Jacob explained.

"We found it lying on the path where it narrows above the gorge." Then, turning to Brigitte, he added, "That gorge was like a raging river." Heidi said nothing, but held the alpenstock close to her, watching Jacob intently as he continued.

"Hans and the others are still up there. They'll keep looking as long as they can. But there's a new storm building over the Falknis. And this one's carrying a heavy load of snow."

Heidi stared blankly at the alpenstock with a look of disbelief. Jacob turned to Brigitte, shrugging his shoulders helplessly. Brigitte responded by gently stroking Heidi's head.

"Heidi—your grandfather told me that if anything happened to him, I should send for your cousins in Luzern. You understand?"

"You can send for them, but he'll be back. I just know he will." Her eyes held no tears, but Heidi's face was set in a grim expression and her lips trembled. She clutched the alpenstock more closely than ever.

"I hope that's so," said Brigitte simply.

"If Grandfather was really gone forever, I'd know. He'll be back." Heidi, still with the alpenstock, quietly entered the Alm-hut, leaving Jacob and Brigitte on the porch shaking their heads sadly.

Chapter XI
THE CAVE

The cave was large and dark. Hazy smoke from a rock fireplace filled the air. The entrance was covered by animal skins, yet from the outside nothing could be seen. Hidden behind rocks, on the upper craggy heights of the mountain, a stranger to the cave could climb right by, unaware of its existence. It was a lonely and deserted place. But inside, the vast cavern showed signs of human life. This was no animal's lair. Pails of water stood beside stacks of nuts and fruit, neatly arranged in a dim corner. The stone walls bore roughly scratched words, some in a foreign tongue with rows of numbers, grouped together like some primitive calendar. On the floor were more animal skins, and on either side of the cave pine branches had been laid, covered with more skins to make two rustic beds. A gaunt, crumpled figure of a man lay on one bed. In the shadows the figure turned slowly, stretching as if to throw off the mantle of sleep. He sat up, moving his arms in a wide circle, searching, but touching nothing but the bare walls. For he was totally blind. It was Grandfather. To his eyes the cave was a great blackness, but his sense of smell suggested the inside of the Alm-hut. But the air was thick with smoke. Could he really be at home? He felt the pine branches beneath him. This wasn't his bed. Had he fallen asleep in a forest? And it was so dark; why was it so dark? Grandfather rubbed his eyes, and the realization of his affliction overwhelmed him. A tear fell down his rough cheeks. His body ached all over and his legs were bruised and swollen. Cuts smarted on his gnarled hands. He racked his memory, trying to recall the past few hours. And then it suddenly all came rushing back; the search, the long journey in the torrential rain, the thunder, the terrifying fall, then nothing but blackness.

"Hello," he called out. "Heidi?"

But there was no answer. And yet Grandfather sensed he was not alone. Somewhere, out there in the dark, someone or something was stirring.

"Where am I? Who's there?" he shouted. "There must be someone there—I can hear you."

Unseen by Grandfather, a grotesque shadow moved slowly over the wall, resting motionless above his bed. Grandfather called out again.

"Why won't you answer me. Who is it?"

Standing by his bed was the Wild Man, looking down on Grandfather but not saying a word.

Chapter XII
THE COUSINS

Some two weeks later, at the Alm-hut, Heidi was packing her few possessions under the watchful supervision of Martha and Tobias, her cousins from Luzern.

As the days went by after Grandfather's apparent death, Brigitte had wrestled with her conscience and finally, after a week of no news, had complied with Grandfather's plan and phoned Luzern. She would gladly have taken Heidi into her home, but she remembered how firm Grandfather's instructions had been, so the phone call was reluctantly made. In the following days Peter, though still limping, helped his father move all the animals from the Alm-hut down to the farmhouse, under Heidi's tearful supervision.

The moving of the animals was the hardest part of all to Heidi, aside from the shock of her grandfather's mysterious disappearance. Her farewell to Bärli and Schwänli the night before had been almost unbearable. But she realized that it was inevitable and that these were her grandfather's wishes. And she was comforted in knowing that the goats, chickens and rabbits would have loving care in their new home, for Peter had promised faithfully to look after them well.

Cousins Martha and Tobias were both in their sixties, and rather stiff and set in their ways. At this stage in their lives they found it difficult to accept responsibility for a young child. In their way, they had been fond of Wilhelm Beck and had made him a promise. They were going to keep their word, however difficult it might be. Cousin Tobias pulled a large silver watch from his waistcoat pocket, and studied it nervously.

"We have a long walk down to the village," he said, carefully replacing the watch. Heidi concluded during their walk down the mountain that looking at his watch was a traditional ritual with Cousin Tobias, for he stopped, removed, studied and put the watch back in his pocket six or seven times. It would have been far easier just to look up at the sun, Heidi thought. Or perhaps Cousin Tobias inspected his watch out of habit.

But the first time the watch appeared, Heidi rapidly responded. "I'm almost ready, Cousin Tobias," she said, fastening up her little hamper.

"Little children don't have the same sense of time as grownups," observed Cousin Martha.

Cousin Tobias proclaimed rather pompously as though he was reading from a church pulpit, "A child who lives in my house will set her clock by mine."

I haven't got a clock, thought Heidi, and anyway if I follow Cousin Tobias, I'll be setting it every ten minutes. She had noticed that not only did Cousin Tobias look at his watch frequently, but he was continually winding and adjusting it. But Heidi kept her thoughts to herself. She looked around the Alm-hut, and seeing the alpenstock lying on her grandfather's chair, picked it up. Heidi had left it on the chair since Jacob had brought it down from the mountain that grey morning.

"Were you thinking of taking that thing with you?" asked Cousin Martha.

"There'll be no use for that in Luzern. Little girls don't climb Pilatus or Rigi," added Cousin Tobias.

"All right, I'll leave it," said Heidi, wishing to avoid a discussion. "When Grandfather comes home, he'll need his alpenstock."

Tobias had been sitting in the rocker, much to Heidi's unspoken disapproval. He leaned forward to reply.

"Wilhelm has no more need of walking sticks."

"Tobias!" scolded Martha.

Tobias began to preach again. "We've been handed responsibility for the child, Martha, and it isn't responsible to encourage false hopes." Tobias rose from the rocker and moved towards Heidi at the table.

"You seem to be a sensible girl, and you must look at things as they are. It's plain to see we have some difficult days ahead of us. It isn't your choice to live with us."

Heidi tried hard not to nod her head in agreement.

"It wasn't our choice to have you," he continued, "but here we are. So all we can do is to make the best of it, all of us. It means adjusting and accommodating. It's easier for the young to change, so most of the burden will be on you."

Heidi gave Cousin Tobias a beautiful smile. She may have forced the smile ever so slightly, but she genuinely wanted to make a good impression on her cousins.

"I want to please you, Cousin Tobias," she said.

"Good," said Tobias sharply. "Time to be on our way."

The three headed for the door. Heidi turned to have a last look around the beloved Alm-hut. Seeing the colorful rug by the fireplace, she ran over and carefully folded it before putting it on her grandfather's rocker. Picking up her basket, she joined her cousins outside, locking the door behind her and placing the key in a secret place behind a little bush. The party started their journey towards Dörfli. The fir trees sang sadly in the winter winds.

Chapter XIII
THE BIG CITY

Heidi walked down the mountain path to Dörfli
more slowly than usual, for the cousins were old
and unaccustomed to rough mountain trails. Every
so often, Tobias stopped and offered to carry
Heidi's wicker suitcase, but Heidi declined the
offer graciously, feeling very protective of her few
belongings.

As they neared the Langes' farmhouse, they met
Peter, who was leaning on the gate, a walking stick
propped against the fence. They all exchanged
greetings, then the cousins moved a little way
down the path, leaving Heidi and Peter a moment
to say their farewells.

"Are you coming down, Peter?"

"I'd rather not," he replied, lifting his ban-
daged foot. "All right?"

Heidi nodded understandingly.

"Don't worry about the animals," Peter assured
her. "I'll take good care of them."

"Give Schwänli a little pat once in a while.
She's spoiled."

Peter changed the subject, looking up towards

the Falknis. "It's all my fault. If only I hadn't got lost. Oh, Heidi, I feel so bad."

"Don't. If you feel bad, I feel bad. Feeling bad doesn't help anyone." She patted his shoulder. Peter took the old compass from around his neck and held it out to Heidi.

"Here. I want you to have this."

"No. I couldn't take your compass, Peter."

"But I want to give you something," he said imploringly.

"You have," said Heidi slowly. "Wiedersehn."

"Wiedersehn, Heidi."

Peter turned and, with his stick, limped quickly towards the house, trying to hide his feelings. Heidi looked after him for a moment, and then ran to join Tobias and Martha.

When they reached the village, the postbus was parked in front of the Alpenrose. Cousin Tobias had explained that the journey would require several changes. The postbus would take them to Bad Ragaz, where they would pick up another bus to Sargans, and then they'd board a train. In normal times, the prospect of such a long journey by bus and train would have excited Heidi tremendously, but today she was sad at leaving the mountain and the village and could not appreciate the trip ahead.

"Well, let's get on the bus," said Tobias.

"Where's the child?" he asked.

"She just ran to the post office to give them a forwarding address, in case she receives a letter," explained Martha.

"A letter? Who would write her a letter? She

has nobody left but us." Tobias was standing by the bus door.

"A friend in Zurich, I believe," said Martha.

Heidi came running down the street towards the bus. "I gave Herr Buhler your address in Luzern," she said, panting.

"Let's get good seats," said Tobias, climbing the bus steps. Martha and Heidi followed him onto the postbus. At that moment a car came roaring up the road leading to Maienfeld, and stopped with a screech of brakes immediately behind the bus. A young girl jumped from the car. "Heidi!" she called. "Heidi!"

It was Elizabeth. Heidi, on the top step of the bus, turned happily, hearing her friend's voice.

"Bet! Bet! You did get my letter!" Heidi climbed down from the bus and hugged Elizabeth. Tobias and Martha, already seated, stared out of the bus window in astonishment. Mady, who was driving the car, got out and joined Elizabeth.

Elizabeth explained breathlessly, "I only got your letter yesterday. There wasn't time to write. So I talked to my father, but he was going off to Brazil and I knew you'd be leaving. Oh, Heidi! I had the most wonderful idea." Elizabeth took Mady's hand and continued, "You remember Mady Roush, my father's secretary."

"Grützi, Fräulein Roush," said Heidi politely. Mady acknowledged Heidi's greeting with some reserve.

"Hello," she said.

Tobias and Martha had now got off the bus

and were watching with puzzled expressions. "You have to get on the bus now, Heidi," Tobias said with some annoyance.

"Are these your Luzern cousins?" asked Mady.

"Yes, Cousin Tobias and Cousin Martha," explained Heidi, introducing them. The cousins shook hands with Mady.

"I'm Madeline Roush, secretary to Herr Wyler of Wyler-Dietrich. And this is Elizabeth, Herr Wyler's daughter." Tobias nodded towards Elizabeth.

"Wyler-Dietrich—the school that trains for hotel work?" he asked Mady.

"That's right. Herr Wyler has sent me to suggest an alternative life-plan for Heidi." Tobias looked at Martha with complete incomprehension. Heidi and Elizabeth had moved away from the others, and the three grownups continued their conversation.

"Do I understand you correctly?" asked Tobias. "You want to take Heidi to Zurich? Why?"

"Herr Wyler is willing to try anything to help Elizabeth," explained Mady, "and hopes that with Heidi as companion—"

Martha interrupted. "She's a child, not a nurse or a maid."

"Since Elizabeth's mother died, she's been more and more withdrawn, more difficult," Mady explained. "Herr Wyler is a busy man—one of the world's busiest. He's put Elizabeth in the best schools, but the only time in three years she's been really happy was when she was with Heidi."

Both Tobias and Martha listened intently as the secretary outlined Dan Wyler's plan. It was, of course, Elizabeth's idea, but Mady was reluctant to admit that, particularly to the Luzern cousins. Tobias frowned, shaking his head.

"We're the child's only relatives," he said. "We have a duty to perform."

Mady reassured him. "Believe me, Herr Wyler will see she has the best."

"It does seem like a wonderful opportunity," said Martha slowly.

"Advantages we certainly can't give her—" Tobias admitted.

"And she'd be happier with someone her own age," added Martha, who was beginning to think of a dozen reasons why Heidi might be better off in Zurich.

Mady continued. "I know Heidi would like to go—so why not let us try? If it doesn't work out in a few weeks, we'll bring her to Luzern and what's been lost?"

"We do want to do what's best for the child," Tobias answered sincerely.

Heidi and Elizabeth were talking animatedly together and laughing. Tobias and Martha looked at each other and then over to the happy children.

"All right. We'll try it," he said.

Tobias drew Heidi to one side and explained the decision he and Martha had reached. Heidi looked up at Cousin Tobias with wide-open eyes. She smiled and put out her hand. "Thank you, Cousin Tobias. It was very kind of you to come and see me. And you, too, Cousin Martha. I know Grandfather will think we're doing the right thing." Tobias shot a quick look at Martha. Then they all shook hands as they said good-byes.

"Wiedersehn—Wiedersehn, Heidi." And the Luzern cousins boarded the bus.

Heidi, Elizabeth and Mady waved at them through the bus window. For a moment, Heidi felt sorry for the old couple, sitting so quietly in the bus. They looked rather sad, she thought. She waved again, then quickly turned and joined Mady and Elizabeth, and they all three got into Mady's car. The car roared off down the Maienfeld road, leaving the bus still parked outside the Alpenrose. Heidi looked back once, and up to the towering Falknis for a last lingering view of what she felt were her mountains. The picture of her grandfather sitting in his rocker puffing his old pipe flashed through her mind, but then it was gone, and she was back with Elizabeth and Mady, tearing through the crisp wintry air, laughing and smiling as the car seemed to devour the road ahead. They passed Sargans, and soon the Zurichsee opened up on their right. The road passed through tunnels in the rock, which were dark and exciting, but quickly they were in the sunlight again, and there was the glistening lake below, with little sailboats skimming the surface like gnats on a great pond. On the far side of the lake were mountains, not as high as the Falknis, but tall and imposing. And Mady knew the names of each peak.

The car flashed through little towns with strange

names like Horgen and Thalwil, and the land grew
flatter as they approached the outskirts of Zurich.
Soon they were in the city itself, where Heidi had
never seen so many people all crowded together.
Like ants on a giant anthill and just as busy. She
didn't know which was the more alarming, the
noisy traffic or the tall, tall buildings. How did all
those cars and trucks avoid hitting each other?
Mady must be a wonderful driver. And those vast
glass-fronted steel mountains rising to the sky.
Why, in Dörfli the tallest house was only three
stories, and that had looked enormous. But scattered in between the monster skyscrapers, Heidi
was relieved to see, were smaller old buildings and
little churches, though dwarfed and cowering beside their modern neighbors.

The car wended its way through an endless
labyrinth of streets and then pulled up outside a
large, sleek apartment complex where, Mady explained, Herr Wyler lived. They passed through
the great glass doors, held open for them by a tall,
stern man in uniform, rather like what Herr Baumes
wore on festival days, thought Heidi. And then
they were in the elevator, silently and rapidly rising to an upper floor. Lights flashed on an indicator above Heidi's head and when the number "15"
appeared the door opened by itself. What a way
to reach the Alm-hut from Dörfli, Heidi was thinking as she followed Mady and Elizabeth down the
richly carpeted hallway.

The apartment door was opened by Herr Wy-

Grandfather (Burl Ives) relaxes with the three children—(*left to right*) Peter (Sean Marshall), Heidi (Katy Kurtzman), and Elizabeth (Sherrie Wills).

Heidi

Heidi and Grandfather

Grandfather in the Alm-hut

Heidi and her best friend, Peter, in the
meadows above the small Swiss village of Dörfli

Peter

Mady (Marlyn Mason, *left*) gives Elizabeth a warm hug as Dan Wyler (John Gavin) turns to thank Grandfather and Heidi for taking care of his runaway daughter.

Heidi sadly packs her few possessions in her wicker suitcase as she prepares to leave the Alm-hut after the disappearance of Grandfather.

Before she is ready to leave the Alm-hut with Cousin
Martha (*center*) and Cousin Tobias (*right*), Heidi
lovingly says good-bye to the wooden figures made
by her grandfather.

"Bet! Bet! You did get my letter!" Heidi embraces
Elizabeth as Mady (*left*) introduces herself to
Cousin Martha and Cousin Tobias and proposes that
Heidi come to live with Elizabeth in Zurich.

ler's houseman, heavyset and in his fifties, wearing
a smart white jacket.

"Guten Tag—Fräulein Roush, Fräulein Elizabeth."

Mady introduced Heidi.

"Oscar—this is Heidi."

"Grützi," said Heidi politely.

"A pleasure, Fräulein Heidi," said Oscar, bowing slightly. "I've prepared the guest room for the
young ladies."

Heidi looked around at the living room with
wondering eyes. She'd never seen, nor could have
imagined, such a spacious "stube." The furniture
was strange and modern looking, rather like ad-
vertisements in a magazine at the Alpenrose with
so many pictures and all those sculptures and
bronze heads. They must be famous people like
Herr Wyler. Her thoughts were interrupted by
Elizabeth.

"This is the apartment my father uses between
planes."

"It's so big," said Heidi solemnly.

Mady explained, "Not designed for children,
but if all goes well, by tomorrow night you'll both
be at school."

Oscar inclined his head to Mady, with a questioning look. "Fräulein Heidi's luggage?"

Mady nodded to the little wicker basket. Heidi
picked up the basket, protectively.

"I can carry it," she said.

"Allow me, Fräulein." Oscar took the basket and

carried it into another room. Heidi watched him, fascinated. For such a large man, he walked so delicately. Perhaps he has sore feet, thought Heidi, or maybe he's trying to protect the carpet.

"Are you girls too tired for shopping?" asked Mady.

"Not me," said Elizabeth.

"I'm not tired at all," said Heidi.

"Well," Mady suggested, "let's find some Zurich clothes for Heidi."

Oscar had returned and, with clasped hands, asked Mady, "Will the young ladies be dining in?"

"No, we'll celebrate Heidi's first night in Zurich by dining out."

Oscar bowed again. "Very well, Fräulein."

As Oscar moved away, Heidi watched his delicate walk, deciding the problem must be with his feet.

"Herr Oscar. Have you ever tried hot mustard poultices?"

Oscar stopped and swiveled gracefully in his tracks. "I beg your pardon, Fräulein?"

Heidi pointed to Oscar's feet. "For your bunions. My grandfather has bunions. He says there's nothing like mustard poultices."

Oscar bowed to Heidi. He had a twinkle in his eye. "I shall keep that in mind, Fräulein."

Returning to the car, which the doorman had delivered to the main entrance of the building, Mady drove the girls through little streets, winding in and out so that Heidi marveled at how well Mady seemed to know her way around this vast, busy city. As she drove, Mady pointed out various places of interest. After twenty minutes or so, Mady parked the car in a side street and walked the girls to a long, broad avenue, planted with lime trees. There were banks, modern buildings and luxury shops. People swarmed the pavements.

"This is the Bahnhofstrasse, Heidi," explained Mady. "Once, many years ago, Zurich was a walled city and this was the Fröschengraben or "Frog's Moat."

Heidi looked up and down the wide street, teeming with people. She couldn't imagine frogs there. She laughed.

Mady continued, "But now the Bahnhofstrasse is one of the world's famous streets, especially for shopping, like the Champs Élysées in Paris, or Bond Street in London, or—" She broke off, realizing that Heidi might not be interested. Heidi was, in fact, fascinated listening to Mady, although she had never heard of all those places.

They spent nearly two hours shopping. Heidi had never seen so many clothes. At first, it was a novelty, trying on many pretty dresses. But after a while, she tired of the ever-polite shop assistants, the rows upon rows of coats, suits and hats, the incessant handshaking, and the repeated comments, "What a lovely little girl," "That color suits her complexion," "That dress is definitely her!"

Heidi was relieved when she heard Mady announce, "That's all for today." They left the last store with Mady carrying two large brightly wrapped packages. During the shopping expedition Elizabeth had watched quietly, but with warm interest, as her new friend from the mountains discarded her country clothes to try on one and yet another smart new outfit.

Now it was getting late, and Mady thought it was time she found them a suitable restaurant. They walked down the Bahnhofstrasse towards the railway station, turning right over the Rudolf Brun bridge and onto the Limmat Quai, a tree-lined street that runs alongside the Limmat River, which joins the lake of Zurich. On the city side of the street are many fine shops and restaurants. Mady steered the girls into the Rotisserie Alexander, and soon they were seated at a large table, with the headwaiter hovering behind them. Heidi marveled at the candlelight, the heavy silverware, the plush chairs and the soft music in the background. A magnificent palace to visit and admire, but Heidi could only think of the Alm-hut with the two chairs by the table and the pitcher of goat's milk. Her thoughts were interrupted by Mady, who was ordering their meal from a large leather-bound book with a red hanging tassle, which Heidi was afraid would dip into her water glass.

After the dishes Mady ordered had been served, they ate silently. Soothing strains of Strauss from the small string orchestra blended with the low hum of conversation from other diners in the large candlelit room. Mady was still eating as both girls, after toying with their food, pushed away their plates. Heidi's mind was far away, lost in the music. She had never heard anything so beautiful, as "Tales from the Vienna Woods" gently wrapped her in dreams. She was on the mountain again, and there was the soft rustle of the wind in the fir trees. As the last notes faded, Mady looked up.

"Elizabeth, your appetite was much better before, when you were with Heidi."

Elizabeth nodded.

"Then what's wrong tonight?" Mady asked.

The two girls glanced at each other.

"It's all this fancy food," said Elizabeth.

"Prepared by some of the best chefs in Switzerland," observed Mady tartly.

"Not nearly as good as homemade bread, cheese and goat's milk," said Elizabeth, giving Heidi a little nudge under the table. Both girls smiled, as though sharing a hidden secret.

Later that night at the Wyler apartment, after Heidi and Elizabeth had gone to bed, the persistent ringing of the telephone woke Oscar, who tiptoed across the living room and picked up the receiver.

"Herr Wyler's residence. Oscar speaking," he said sleepily. "Just one moment, sir."

Mady had appeared at the door.

"For you, Fräulein Roush, the master."

Mady took the phone from Oscar, who silently and gladly went back to bed.

"Yes, this is Madeline Roush. Yes, I can hear you."

Although the line crackled and the sound wavered, Madeline could hear Dan Wyler's voice clearly. He was calling from the Copacabana Palace in Rio de Janeiro.

"I wanted to check up on your progress as nursemaid and governess."

"That was very thoughtful of you, sir," answered Mady.

"How's it going?" asked Dan.

"I put them to bed an hour ago. We shopped and had dinner at Alexander's. Heidi was not impressed."

There was a moment's pause, then Dan asked, "Is it going to work?"

"I'll bet against it, sir."

"I have the feeling you don't want it to work," responded Dan.

"I follow orders."

"Of course. But what do you think personally?" Dan asked persistently. Mady was now fully awake and she moved to the sofa, taking the phone with her.

"Personally, I think you've gone too far this time. For three years, you've been trying to cope with Elizabeth by giving her everything she's asked for. But five minutes after she has what she said she wanted, she's dissatisfied. What she really wants is your undivided attention—and that's just not available—at any price . . ."

"Somehow—this seemed different," Dan answered slowly.

"It is," she said. "Buying a dog, a house or a speedboat and then discarding them is one thing.

But using another human being in the same way is heartless."

"Is Heidi unhappy?" Dan asked.

"I don't think so—but it's difficult to tell."

There was a pause, then the conversation turned to business matters for a few minutes.

"Well, keep me informed and get a good night's sleep." Then he hung up.

Nearby, in the luxurious guest room, with its two large beds, Elizabeth was sleeping. In the next bed, Heidi was still awake, staring at the dancing shadow patterns on the ceiling. It had been an eventful day but now, fighting sleep, she was overcome with a feeling of loneliness, despite the presence of her friend.

Heidi whispered, "Good night—Grandfather."

Her unhappiness faded and she closed her eyes.

Heidi slept, and the city's roar was dimmed.

Far, far away from Zurich, beyond the rolling Toggenburg, and across the valley of the Rhine, in the craggy region where the mighty Falknis reaches for the sky, an old man lay in a dark mountain cave searching for sleep. In flickering shadows cast by the glow of a waning fire, another figure, long-haired and disheveled, sat hunched on the floor staring silently at the last burning embers. All was quiet within the cave. Outside a lonely bird cried in the wind, disturbing the peace of an Alpine night.

Chapter XIV
THE SCHOOL

Nordstrom School lies in one of the older residential districts of Zurich. Shortly after the First World War, multimillionaire Bjorn Nordstrom built a beautiful mansion on the estate in what was then the newest, most fashionable district of this fast growing city. Even in those days the magnificent building, with its stables, tennis courts and gardens, must have cost a small fortune. Ten years after the house was completed, the wealthy widower died, and he bequeathed the entire estate to a trust that was instructed to establish a girls' school. The school was in memory of his wife and the children they had never had. Bjorn Nordstrom had always prayed for a little girl and now, ironically, many years after his death, the estate he had built and loved rang with the echoes of girlish laughter and animated talk from young ladies of many nations. Nordstrom School for Girls was now one of the most famous and most expensive establishments of its kind and truly international in its choice of pupils. Parents, however rich, could not automatically enroll their children. The members of the board and especially the headmistress decided who was to be chosen to enter the iron gates and to be privileged to study within those walls.

On this crisp, wintry morning, the principal, Madame Lemay, was sitting behind her imposing walnut desk interviewing a prospective student. Heidi stood before the headmistress with her hands held behind her back. She could just see over the top of the massive desk. Mady was sitting in a leather armchair and attentively listening to the interview.

The very nature of the room, with its booklined walls, dark antique furniture and heavy curtains, would have been enough to intimidate all but the most stalwart of applicants. Madame Lemay herself was a forbidding-looking woman in her forties, with the disconcerting habit of balancing her pince-nez on the very tip of her nose. Every so often these gold-rimmed glasses lost their grip on her aquiline feature and were only prevented from clattering to the desk by the velvet ribbon to which they were attached and which Madame Lemay wore around her birdlike neck. Heidi, although intrigued by this repeated balancing trick, stood her ground and answered the principal's questions in a steady, clear voice.

Madame Lemay, having readjusted her glasses, at least temporarily, and after scrutinizing Heidi for what seemed an eternity, asked, "And how many years have we attended school?"

"This is my fourth," answered Heidi.

"So, we do read and write."

"Oh, yes," she said politely.

Madame Lemay continued, "I think the wisest procedure would be to place you temporarily on our first level. After testing, we'll have a clearer picture of your capabilities." At this point the glasses dropped once more, and Madame Lemay took longer than usual to replace them. She motioned to Heidi.

"Now, would you wait out there while I have a few words with Fräulein Roush."

Madame Lemay indicated the French windows, half hidden behind the drapes. Heidi, with a sigh of relief that the interview was over, opened the glass doors and stepped into the garden. Before her lay a stretch of open lawn, a carpet of well-tended green surrounded by herbaceous borders and a neat, freshly trimmed hedge. Taking a deep breath, Heidi contemplated the scene, feeling this was the nearest to the countryside she had been since leaving the mountain. Then her eye caught the figure of an old man, bending over a flower bed on the far side of the lawn. His attitude and movements together with the white hair and beard made Heidi's heart thump. Grandfather! What was her grandfather doing in this school garden? She ran joyously across the lawn.

"Grandfather! Grandfather!" she called.

The old man, on hearing her cries of delight, straightened his back and turned to the little girl who was running towards him. As he turned, Heidi suddenly stopped, her eyes opening wide in an expression of both surprise and disappointment. From a distance the old man looked like Grandfather, but up close he seemed smaller, and his face bore no resemblance to her grandfather's. A warm, kind face—yes, but not her grandfather's.

"I'm sorry," Heidi faltered.

"No—I'm sorry," the old man said. "It's true I'm a grandfather—but not yours. Are you just starting school here?"

Heidi gazed at the friendly old face before answering.

"Well, yes—if they accept me."

The old gardener chewed a long grass stalk as he looked at Heidi quizzically. "You're smaller than most," he said. "What's your name?"

"Heidi—Heidi Beck."

"Heidi," the old man repeated. "Well, 'pon my soul, that's a pretty name. Makes me feel good just to say it. I'm Junius . . . Junius Schmidt."

Heidi grasped his outstretched hand. "Grützi—Herr Schmidt," she said.

"Junius—please," he insisted, then continued. "As far as I'm concerned, you're accepted here!"

"Thank you," said Heidi smiling. "Do you have an important job here?"

"Well, I look after the garden." Junius waved his hand at the vast expanse of lawns and flower beds. "And I keep up the furnaces, help with the horses —and—" He paused.

"They just couldn't get along without you," said

Heidi brightly, then looking at the beds where Junius had been planting bulbs, offered, "Can I help you?"

"Don't want you to get dirty," Junius replied, smiling.

"Oh, I'll be careful," said Heidi.

Junius nodded, and the old man and his little assistant bent down and busied themselves with the spring bulbs.

Inside, behind the heavy drapes, Madame Lemay and Mady continued their talk.

Madame Lemay tapped a book with the pince-nez. "Fräulein Roush, I want to emphasize," each word being accompanied by a tap, "that we are only enrolling the child tentatively, and even that is an expression of regard for Herr Wyler."

Madame Lemay recognized Dan Wyler as an important businessman and had not forgotten the special terms he had arranged with the supplier of provisions to the school's kitchens.

"We appreciate that," said Mady.

"I'm very much afraid the girl's too immature to respond to our curriculum." Madame Lemay tapped her glasses. "But we shall see. We'll place her in a room with Elizabeth and two other girls."

Mady, realizing her mission was accomplished, stood up and extended her hand. "Danke schön, Madame Lemay," she said. Then, opening the French windows, she saw in the distance Heidi and the old gardener bending over a flower bed.

"Heidi!" Mady called.

On hearing her name, Heidi jumped up and,

fter a quick look towards Mady, turned to Junius. "I must be going, Junius—Wiedersehn." They olemnly shook hands, but not before Junius had arefully wiped his hand on his blue apron.

"Wiedersehn—Heidi. Thanks for helping out."

Then Heidi cheerfully ran across the lawn to Mady.

Chapter XV
SCHOOL FRIENDS

As Madame Lemay promised, Heidi was given a
room arranged for four girls. A few days later when
she arrived with Mady at her new living quarters
the room was empty, giving Heidi the opportunity
to look around before her roommates arrived.

The room was large and airy, with four beds
each covered with a brightly colored patchwork
quilt. Above each bed was a pine night table with
a reading lamp decorated with Alpine flowers. On
the other side of each bed were a desk and chair
Heidi liked her first impression of the room, par
ticularly the floral lamp shades, though she couldn'
help thinking of the Alm-hut loft, where her grand
father had forbidden her to take an oil lamp o
light a candle for fear of fire.

Rugs covered the well-polished wooden floor
and over each bed the girls had placed ornament
and pictures, giving each corner a little of the occu
pant's own individuality. Hers must be the bed
with no pictures, and the one next to it Heidi
recognized as Elizabeth's, with pictures of what
must be German or Swiss "Film-schauspielers," o

actors, probably torn from the weekly *Stern* magazine. Beside the movie stars Heidi noticed a faded and creased snapshot of a beautiful young woman holding a baby and wondered whether this was Elizabeth's mother. Leading off from the bedroom was a door that Heidi found led to a bathroom, and she admired with delight four separate towel racks, each with different colored towels. Returning to Mady, who was standing by Heidi's bed, she put down her little wicker basket. Mady seemed anxious to leave.

"Bet will be coming along soon from class. I really should be getting back to the office—"

"I'll be fine. Wiedersehn, Fräulein Roush," said Heidi.

Wishing her good luck with a parting "Viel Glück," Mady left Heidi alone in her new surroundings.

Heidi put her basket on the quilt and unpacked her clothes, which she folded neatly in the drawers of the nightstand. She had left two of her new Zurich dresses at the Wyler apartment because Mady had told her that apart from underclothes and nightwear she would only need the uniform that the school provided. Her unpacking completed, Heidi looked at the empty wall space above her bed and wondered where in the world she'd find pictures to fill the space. And if she did, what pictures did she want? If only she had a photo of her grandfather, but, as far as she knew, he'd never had his picture taken. And then Heidi remembered the old photo hanging in the Alpenrose of a group of villagers, most wearing beards, representing the Dörfli rifle team. The shooters had all looked proud; but prouder than all of them sat the Alm-Uncle in the center, holding his rifle and a silver cup. He'd looked younger then, thought Heidi, so the picture must have been taken years ago.

But if she could have had a photograph of her grandfather, Heidi would have wanted one as she remembered him best, sitting back in his own rocker and puffing that old carved pipe. As she formed the picture of her grandfather in her mind, Heidi could almost smell his rough-burning tobacco and hear the familiar squeak of his chair as Grandfather rocked gently.

Turning away from the bed and the thoughts of home that kept flooding her memory, Heidi noticed what appeared to be a number of metal rings lying on the rug by the opposite bed. The rings were all joined together and, picking them up, she decided it was a puzzle and the challenge was to separate them. She sat on the edge of the bed, turning the rings this way and that, until suddenly, with a metallic click, the rings separated.

Heidi was overjoyed that she had solved the puzzle and put back the rings neatly, side by side, on the bed.

At that moment, two girls burst into the room. The fatter of the two, who Heidi later learned was called Lisl, carried a paper bag from a bakery and was closely followed by Natalie, who was frowning.

"What did you do with my puzzle?" Natalie shouted at Heidi. She snatched up the separated rings from the bed and flung them into a nightstand drawer.

"They were on the floor—" Heidi started to explain. Meanwhile, plump Lisl had opened the bakery bag and, sitting on the bed, was munching two cakes at once, one in each hand. Lisl looked up at Natalie and, with her mouth full of cake, mumbled, "Hey, Natalie—she worked out the puzzle."

This comment, though garbled, gave Natalie an even greater cause for annoyance. "What's happening to this school?" she exclaimed bitterly. "Any little brat can walk in off the street and pick up a person's private property—and—" Natalie was lost for further words to express her indignation.

"I didn't walk in off the street," said Heidi simply. "I'm going to live here with you."

"Oh, no!" spluttered Natalie angrily. "You must be Elizabeth's goatherd. That explains the peculiar smell."

Having rapidly demolished two cakes, Lisl looked at Heidi, then came over and shook hands.

"I'm Lisl. What's your name?"

"Heidi."

This was too much for Natalie, and seemed to further increase her irritability. "Heidi! That's no proper name," she said rudely.

"It's worked all right for ten years," replied Heidi calmly.

"Touché," said Lisl, offering Heidi the bakery bag. "Would you like a cake?"

Natalie, not wishing to spare anyone from her bad humor, turned abruptly on Lisl. "You're changing into a cake yourself, Lisl."

Lisl, ignoring the remark, continued to talk to Heidi, making pretense of politely and formally introducing Natalie. "This charming girl is Natalie. She's also known as Mademoiselle Bad Mouth, Spider Woman. The girl you love to hate," she said sarcastically.

Ignoring Lisl completely, Natalie continued to vent her bad temper on Heidi. "Well, if we're going to have you with us, you might as well be useful. You'll make my bed, clean my part of the bathroom and be available to run errands, is that understood?"

Anyone else might have wilted under this barrage of orders, but Heidi remained calm and replied quietly, "I'll do any of those things for you —if you ask me as a friend."

Natalie was, for the moment, nonplussed.

Lisl quickly volunteered, "Natalie hasn't had a friend since she learned to talk."

"I'll do anything as a friend," Heidi repeated. "But I won't be your servant."

"Then you won't be with us long," retorted Natalie.

At that moment the confrontation between Natalie and Heidi was interrupted by Elizabeth, who came in with an armful of schoolbooks. She looked at Heidi. "Heidi—what's going on?"

Lisl giggled. "Natalie just wrecked the Welcome Committee."

Elizabeth, with her arm around Heidi, drew her away from Natalie, fearing that her first encounter with the bad-tempered girl would cause Heidi to have second thoughts about staying with her at Nordstrom.

"Don't pay any attention to her," said Elizabeth. "Or to any of them. It's just the two of us. Just you and me."

But Natalie was going to have the last word. "And when things get really rough, you can both run away." With that, Natalie strode to the bathroom, slamming the door.

The other three girls looked at each other, smiling, and Heidi felt they could all be friends. Heidi lay back on her bed, reflecting on her first meeting with her new roommates. She looked across at Elizabeth and winked. Elizabeth winked back.

A few days later, Heidi attended her first class in composition, conducted by a Fräulein Eames and held in a large modern classroom on the main floor. The teacher reminded Heidi of her Aunt Gritli. She was about the same age, and her looks were similar, though perhaps more birdlike. Fräulein Eames had a precise and learned manner, but her most prominent feature was her nose, which was sharp and aquiline. Almost like a beak, thought Heidi, suppressing a giggle.

Sitting next to Elizabeth, she looked round the class and saw her other two roommates in different rows farther back. The teacher and class were now listening to a girl named Heather as she read her composition. Most lessons were conducted in German, though there were selected classes in English and French. Although she spoke German, Fräulein Eames seemed to prefer French, as she kept making little comments and asides in that language. Heidi couldn't decide whether she was really French or whether she used the language to impress the class with her abilities and international background. Heather was standing by her desk and reading from a notebook. Heidi decided she was very well named, as Heather was delicate looking with deep blue eyes. She couldn't have been called Rose, thought Heidi, remembering the beautiful sturdy red and white blossoms in the gardens at Dörfli.

Heather read with a clear, high voice.

> *"As we stood, on that sunny spring day, among the wild flowers and ancient marble columns of the Acropolis, I felt I knew a little of what it must have been like as a Greek girl over 2,000 years ago."*

Heather sat down amid a murmur of appreciation and envy from the class.

Fräulein Eames preened herself and pronounced her judgment on Heather's reading.

"Excellent, really excellent, Heather," she said. "You made me feel I was there with you—and that's true communication. Whom shall we hear from next? Heidi—are you prepared?"

"Yes, Fräulein Eames," said Heidi, rising. She wasn't sure she could compete with Heather, but she had decided to tell the class about what she knew. The night before in her room she had made notes for today's class, in the event she was called upon.

"I would like to tell you about my grandfather—" started Heidi.

Natalie, in a whisper audible throughout the classroom, interrupted, "Her grandfather! Now, that's an exotic experience."

There was subdued tittering from the class.

Heidi paused for a moment, then continued. "I live with him in a cottage on the Alm above Dörfli. We have four goats—"

Natalie again interrupted, though this time the whisper was louder. "She knows what it's like to be a goat! Baaaa!"

The giggling from the class increased, and Heidi was becoming puzzled and distressed. Fräulein Eames rapped on her desk in an attempt to restore order.

"Mesdemoiselles!" she cried. "*S'il vous plaît*—"

But the giggling continued.

Realizing that the teacher's entreaty for quiet was going unheeded, Heidi determined to take the matter into her own hands and, planting her feet firmly while looking around at her classmates, continued.

"We were asked to write about something we know well and try to share it. I've never been to an opera, but I was glad to hear Kristi tell about

The Magic Flute. I've never been to Greek ruins, but I learned something from Heather. None of you has ever had my kind of life. Won't you let me tell you about it?"

As Heidi spoke, the giggling ceased, and the class, including Natalie, sat in stunned silence. Fräulein Eames, relieved that Heidi had succeeded where she had failed, broke the hush that had descended on the room.

"Heidi is quite right, listening to others is a skill and an art." She continued, "It's only the limited and immature girl who thinks no other life-style is as interesting as hers. Heidi, please go on."

Heidi looked round the classroom, smiling. The other girls smiled back as a sign of encouragement. Heidi knew she now held her audience and she spoke with greater confidence.

"We have two pet goats and six more counting Peter's. They all have names, except one. He's called 'No-Name.'"

The girls were laughing now, but they were laughing with Heidi. Elizabeth listened intently to her friend, gazing at Heidi proudly as she told about her grandfather and life at the Alm-hut.

"My grandfather is like the mountains. From far away he looks stern and frightening, but the closer you get, the more gentleness and goodness you can see."

The class was entranced as Heidi described Dörfli and the mountain path up the Falknis. Her words were simple, but they brought the village and the mountain to life. They could imagine

Peter and his parents' farm; they could see the clouds over the peaks and feel the wind in the fir trees. For a while they lived a life they had never known.

Heidi's last words were drowned by the harsh ringing of the bell, telling that class was over. Yet even after the bell had ceased, for a few moments they sat hushed, as if unwilling to break the spell. And then, their dreams over, they grasped their books and poured out into the sunshine of the world outside.

As the weeks went by, Heidi became more and more accustomed to life at Nordstrom. She was genuinely interested in her classes, and her teachers reported to Madame Lemay that she was making good progress, was adapting well and had become an industrious student who was quick to learn. After her first day, life in the little dormitory became more settled, although Natalie from time to time disturbed her. Heidi tried to remain calm. There were moments when Heidi would think back to the Alm-hut and her grandfather, but these memories were becoming less frequent as Heidi became more and more absorbed in the new and busy routine of life at the school. She still missed her animals and, whenever possible, visited the stables, where sometimes she found Junius grooming the horses.

One afternoon, on passing the stables, she saw, through the open doors, the old gardener busily working on a beautiful chestnut mare. She poked her head round the stable door.

"What's her name, Junius?"

"Cinnamon Toast," the old man answered. "Isn't she a beauty? Come in and get acquainted."

Heidi walked carefully over the thick straw and stood quietly on one side of the mare, as Junius continued his work. There was silence for a few minutes, save for an occasional snort from Cinnamon Toast and the sound of Junius blowing through his teeth. He had explained to Heidi that every time he made a stroke with the large bristled brush he made sure of blowing out air from his mouth. In this way he didn't inhale any of the dust from the horse's coat.

"Here, you try it," said Junius, handing Heidi the brush. Heidi gently brushed the mare's golden flanks, puffing out as she brushed.

"That's it—but harder," said Junius approvingly.

Heidi brushed and puffed with more energy for several minutes.

"You're very quiet today, Heidi," said Junius. Heidi didn't reply.

"Want to talk about it?" asked Junius, picking up a piece of straw.

"There's nothing to say," said Heidi, continuing her work on Cinnamon Toast. Junius chewed the straw, watching Heidi.

"Aren't you happy here?" he asked.

"Most of the time." Heidi's words came haltingly between her puffs. Junius spoke slowly, as if to himself.

"Except when you think about Dörfli . . . and your grandfather." Heidi nodded and patted the mare affectionately, resting her cheek against the horse's neck. Cinnamon Toast in return did her best to nuzzle her. Heidi looked up. At the door stood Madame Lemay, looking at Heidi and Junius in a disapproving manner.

"Heidi," said Madame Lemay, "we do not train our young ladies to become stablehands."

Junius, raising his eyebrows, stepped back, trying to make himself invisible in the shadows of the stall.

But Madame Lemay's attention was on Heidi.

"Madame," Heidi replied, "I'm learning to ride horses and—"

"Equitation—yes," Madame Lemay observed tartly.

"It seems to me," Heidi said, "that part of that learning is to take care of the horse I ride."

Madame Lemay pursed her lips and continued, "An interesting connection—I admit. But not one that most of our young ladies will care to take."

"Are you saying I mustn't groom Cinnamon Toast any more?" Heidi persisted.

Madame Lemay relented slightly.

"If you really enjoy it—I won't forbid it," she answered, adding as an afterthought, "but I do not approve."

With that, Madame Lemay turned sharply on her heels and bustled out, leaving Heidi and Junius grinning at each other.

Later that afternoon, Heidi had changed into the smart riding habit that Mady had bought her in Zurich and was waiting for her weekly riding lesson. Other girls, including Elizabeth, were standing by the riding ring as Junius led out a proud Cinnamon Toast, now freshly saddled and bridled.

"Hello, Cinnamon Toast," called Heidi, as Junius and the mare approached.

Natalie, also in riding clothes, pushed brusquely past Heidi and towards Junius, who was now holding Cinnamon Toast in the center of the ring.

"I'm next," she shouted.

"But I've been waiting, Natalie," said Heidi.

"This horse is far too spirited for someone who's used to riding goats," flashed back Natalie, grabbing the reins from the reluctant Junius and putting her left foot in the irons. No sooner had she established a foothold than Cinnamon Toast reared in the air. Natalie disengaged her foot rapidly and jumped back. Not to be outdone, she tried again and again, but each time the mare reared, this last time even more spiritedly, and Natalie found herself lying on her back. Junius recovered the reins and steadied the stirrups, which by now were swinging wildly. Junius grinned as he handed the reins to Heidi, who had been standing quietly in the ring, enjoying Natalie's equestrian demonstration with suppressed delight. Heidi stroked the mare's neck, talking to her in soft tones. Then she easily swung into the saddle and, holding the reins tightly, urged Cinnamon Toast into a smart trot.

A round of applause greeted Heidi as she moved the mare into a rousing canter, and as she did so, no one noticed Natalie as she stalked away, her frown even deeper than usual.

Later that night, in the girls' room, Lisl sat on her bed absorbed in her macramé work. The room looked more cozy since the day, a few weeks before, when Mady had brought Heidi to the dormitory. Elizabeth had added new film star pictures to her collection, and over Heidi's bed were several magazine pictures of animals and Alpine flowers, together with scenes from a Swissair calendar given her by Lisl. In these past weeks Lisl had lost several kilos and was looking trimmer and healthier. Her concentration on the macramé was broken as Natalie entered. Natalie put down her books on her bed and turned to Lisl.

"What's the matter with you?" she asked sharply.

"Take that up with any one of my three therapists," replied Lisl smugly, putting down her work.

"But you're not eating," persisted Natalie.

"I can't believe it either."

"Well, why aren't you eating? And why are you doing that?" Natalie pointed to the macramé with a sneer.

"Well, you see," explained Lisl, "I made a deal with Heidi. Instead of reaching for a cake, I pick up my macramé."

"That's absolutely ridiculous," retorted Natalie.

"Maybe—but it works."

Natalie abandoned her efforts to aggravate Lisl and turned to the desk beside Heidi's bed. "Stupid little meddler," she muttered. From Heidi's desk she picked up a piece of drawing paper on which there was a simple watercolor depicting Heidi's memory of the Alm-hut and the mountain. Although overly colorful and naive, the painting had a certain charm, and Natalie was fascinated despite herself.

Lisl, watching her, tried to divert her attention, at the same time coming to the defense of Heidi, whom she admired.

"Natalie—who worked the puzzle first?" asked Lisl. Natalie did not answer, but, putting the watercolor down on Heidi's desk, picked up a glass of water from the desk top and deliberately spilled it over the picture.

"Natalie!" cried Lisl in alarm.

At that moment Heidi and Elizabeth burst through the door. Elizabeth was talking with excitement in her voice.

"—and then we can skate as long as we like and then go out for a special meal and—" She broke off as both she and Heidi saw the watery mess on Heidi's desk.

Heidi quickly picked up the soggy watercolor, seeing it was ruined. Without a word, Heidi started to mop up the pool of water.

The other three girls looked at each other, not knowing what to say. Lisl tried to ease the awkward pause.

"It was an accident," she said.

But Natalie was determined to take advantage of the situation.

"Some people just can't take a hint. They stay on and on where they're not wanted."

The color in Elizabeth's cheeks rose as she angrily addressed Natalie. "The only person in this room who isn't wanted is you, Natalie."

Lisl chipped in. "Bet and I wanted to have you moved out, but Heidi stood up for you."

This united stand against her was too much for Natalie, and she trembled with rage and frustration. With an outraged cry, she ran out of the room. The little reading lamps shook with the slamming of the door.

Lisl and Elizabeth started to help Heidi clean up the sodden desk.

"Don't worry, Heidi," comforted Lisl, "she's better out of the way."

"But I really wanted to be her friend," Heidi said sadly.

Chapter XVI
THE SKATING RINK

Just outside Zurich, near the lake and on the road to Zollikon, is a beautiful open-air skating rink. On this winter morning the sun was bright, though the cool air encouraged the onlookers to keep wrapped in their winter coats, and the skaters protected their ears with brightly knitted woolen caps.

For weeks Elizabeth had begged her father to let her take Heidi skating on a weekend when they could come home from school. On several Sundays Mady had taken the girls on little excursions, once to the zoo, and once to Kloten airport, where standing on the visitors lookout gallery with Elizabeth and Mady, Heidi had been enthralled by the sight and thundering sounds of the giant jets as they took off and landed. But now Dan Wyler was back in the city, and here they were, joining the dozens of skaters as they whirled round the rink to the stirring and romantic music pouring from the loudspeakers. Sometimes they skated hand in hand, then skated apart, trying out different figures on the shining ice. Heidi was quickly becoming an expert, despite the fact that she had had little practice, except for one or two days in Dörfli when the schoolyard had been frozen over, and those who could borrow skates had joined the fun. The main winter sport in the village, as in most of the rural areas, had been skiing and, as soon as she could walk, Heidi remembered gliding down the mountain slopes. But that was long ago, and the skis were now too small, having been a present from her Aunt Gritli when she was very young.

When Heidi had moved to the Alm-hut she never replaced the skis, and she had not wanted to remind her grandfather that he was too old for such pastimes. But although she had not skied for several years, the feeling of movement and balance was still there, and the transition to skates was quickly made.

As the two girls skimmed round and round the rink, Daniel Wyler and Mady sat in the open-air restaurant enjoying hot chocolate and watching the skaters.

"What are the odds against it working now?" Dan asked Mady.

"I underestimated Heidi," Mady replied thoughtfully.

"And maybe also Elizabeth's feelings for her," Dan added.

"Christmas is coming—"

Dan looked up. "Well, thanks for bringing that to my attention."

"The last two years, Christmas went by without your noting."

Elizabeth and Heidi skated up the terrace and,

holding onto the rail, interrupted the subject of the coming holidays.

"Come on and skate." Elizabeth looked at her father.

Dan smiled. "You're both too good," he said.

"We'll teach you, Herr Wyler," pleaded Heidi.

"Next time," said Dan.

As the two girls skated away, Dan turned to Mady.

"I should figure out something for Heidi to call me instead of Herr Wyler," he mused.

"Like 'father'?" suggested Mady.

Dan frowned and Mady continued, "Sooner or later, you'll have to take some sort of steps towards formal adoption."

"But she still believes her grandfather's alive," protested Dan. Mady leaned forward on the table, touching Dan's arm.

"Dan, it's been weeks since he disappeared."

"I know," said Dan wearily. "But when Heidi says he's alive, don't you believe it?"

Mady nodded unhappily, staring vacantly at the swirling colored mass of circling figures.

Beyond the lake, gleaming in the sunlight, rose the mountains, proud and timeless.

From the loudspeakers came the lilting strains of "The Skater's Waltz." The whirling throng of skaters seemed lost in the music, as a dark cloud passed over the winter sun.

Chapter XVII
THE FÖHN

Far beyond the Zurichsee, way, way up in another world, the snow had been falling steadily for several weeks. In that mysterious region of craggy rocks beneath the peaks of the giant Falknis, a deep blanket of white now covered the rough face of the mountain. The land was wild and lonely, lost between earth and sky.

Now the snow had ceased, and the scattered fir trees, heavy with silver fleece, bowed in the wind, the sparkling crystals from their branches falling like tears on the heavy shimmering carpet of white. Despite weeks of icy cold, the mountain was now caressed by a warmer wind. Trickles of melting snow crept down the steep slopes, and tapering icicles, clinging to the rock face, wept. In the deep of winter the Föhn, that dreaded Alpine wind, had struck the mountain. At the first sign of this warmer wind originating on the northern slopes the people of the Alps became alerted to possible torrents and avalanches ahead. At such times in the valley, the Föhn brought a feeling of depression to the most hardened villagers, who often complained of severe headaches as the warm wind swept down the lower slopes.

But within the cave hidden in the depths of the upper rocks, all was dark and still, and the Föhn was an unknown mystery of the outside world.

To the Alm-Uncle, sitting motionless on his rough bed, all signs of days, weeks or months had vanished. Daytime and nighttime were as one. All was nothing, lost in blackness. Only an occasional feeling of cold or warmth. He loosened the animal skins wrapped around his shoulders, as a warmer breeze enveloped him. The skins covering the entrance to the cave had been pulled aside as the Wild Man entered. Grandfather could hear his footsteps over the steady dripping of the icicles outside.

The Wild Man dropped another log on the meager fire, shivering, although he too had felt the caress of the warmer wind. Grandfather spoke to the dark.

"I began to feel you weren't coming back or couldn't come back. What happens to me then? I just lie here and starve?"

The Wild Man did not answer, but silently placed a wooden dish in Grandfather's hands. Grandfather sniffed the offered food then, tearing a small piece of meat with his fingers, tasted it. Thank goodness it wasn't rabbit again. He'd eaten enough rabbit the last few weeks to last a lifetime. He chewed the meat slowly. It was Bündnerfleisch, smoked dried beef.

"Good," he said, "very good."

The Wild Man did not answer. Grandfather persisted in an effort to make the strange man speak.

"Why did you bring me here at all? Not for company. You never say a word. Maybe you can't. What kind of a life is this? Darkness. Silence. I could get it over quickly with—" Grandfather half rose to his feet, and the Wild Man backed away from him. "I could stumble out here right now and perhaps freeze to death." He paused. "Except that today it seems a little warmer." He waved his arm weakly in the direction of the cave entrance, from where he'd felt the milder breeze.

"Is the Föhn blowing?" he asked.

Not a word from the Wild Man. Grandfather sank back in his bed, muttering into the dark.

"No—I'm still clinging to life, such as it is. For Heidi's sake. That's funny, for what good am I to Heidi or anyone else? Why didn't you leave me where you found me? It'd be over. I want it to be over." Grandfather lay back. A heavy dullness filled his head, pressing on his temples.

Mutely, the Wild Man stood over him, gazing with compassion at the motionless figure of the gaunt stranger.

Outside the wind howled, soft and threatening. Waves of powdered snow lashed the rocks, snapping the dripping icicles. It was a night of the Föhn.

Chapter XVIII
THE END OF TERM

Despite the approaching Christmas holidays, the offices of Wyler-Dietrich were as busy as usual. Somehow, Mady had found time to decorate a small tree, though it was past nine o'clock the night before when the last card had been placed on the tree's branches.

Mady wished she collected postage stamps, because the Christmas cards added to the thousands of exotic foreign stamps that she carefully tore from envelopes throughout the year. She had always meant to give the stamps to her niece in Basle, who would surely appreciate them more than Elizabeth, who would probably be reminded of her father's world travels and his neglect of his only daughter.

At that moment Dan Wyler's buzzer disturbed her thoughts and Mady, steno pad in hand, left her desk, responding to the summons.

Dan's office was large and expensively furnished. All the pictures and office mementos related to his work, and there was little or no evidence of his personal life. Photos of world-famous hotels, framed menus and autographed portraits of chefs and catering executives lined the walls. There was no mistaking Dan's interests. This was the office of a successful executive in the hotel business.

Dan looked up from his desk as Mady entered and sat down, balancing her notebook on her knees.

"New York, the twenty-third. The afternoon flight on Swissair."

Mady was making notes. "An emergency?" she asked.

"The Waldorf. André's turning the kitchen into a disaster area."

"When will you be back?"

"Leave it open—" Dan was looking at his desk diary.

"But—Christmas?"

"Every year there's something," said Dan wearily.

Mady put down her notebook and, looking at Dan, said firmly, "Elizabeth and Heidi are counting on having the holidays with you."

Dan's reply sounded impersonal and business-like. "Can't be helped," he said. "They'll have to stay at the school. They have each other for company. It won't be bad—" His voice trailed off as he thumbed through some papers and placed several files in his briefcase.

"A deserted school—" Mady was appealing to Dan's conscience, though she knew it would be of little avail.

"Maybe you could take them out for Christmas

dinner." Dan was still occupied with his briefcase.

"You've forgotten," said Mady. "I'll be in Berne with my family. You and the girls were invited for the day."

Dan looked up. "Oh, yes. Sorry. I'll just have to do something special when I get back—after all—" His mind seemed far away, but Mady was persistent.

"Don't say it," she said firmly.

"It's true—there will be other Christmases." Dan snapped his briefcase shut with an air of finality, as though he considered the subject closed.

"That's not the point," Mady said adamantly. "You can never have this Christmas back."

Dan looked at her with surprise. "You're angry."

"Usually you don't notice," retorted Mady, firmly closing her notebook. She strode to the door, thought for a moment about slamming it, then changed her mind.

Dan Wyler looked at the closed door, then, with a shrug of his shoulders, returned to work.

The school term was over at Nordstrom, and on this bleak December day there was a bustle of activity as cars drove up the wide gravel entrance way and parents and chauffeurs picked up the girls waiting on the main steps. There was a buzz of excited chatter as each girl, recognizing a familiar Rolls or Mercedes, bade their farewells and Christmas greetings before leaving on their long-awaited holidays. There was much hugging and embracing and the air was filled with cries of

"Merry Christmas," "Joyeux Noël," and "Fröhlich Weihnacht!" Most of the girls were still wearing their school uniforms, though a few had changed into smart outfits.

Standing a little aside from the main cluster on the steps were two girls, still dressed in uniform, holding hands and gazing wistfully at the stream of arriving cars. But Heidi and Elizabeth were by no means neglected by their departing school friends as, almost without exception, each girl, before leaving, came over and greeted them, with Heidi in particular receiving warm hugs and cheerful "Wiedersehn's." She had never felt such affection from so many people in her life, and this warm feeling almost made up for the prospect of spending the next few weeks, including Christmas, in the deserted school. But she would still be with Bet, and at the thought, Heidi gave Elizabeth's hand an extra squeeze.

For in the past months, Heidi, without fully realizing it, had achieved an amazing change in the attitude of nearly all the girls towards her. Natalie might have been the exception, but Heidi still hoped that next term things would be different between them. When she had arrived at the school with Mady, she had felt, and been looked down upon, as a stranger. To the other girls, who for the most part were from wealthy, sophisticated families who had traveled extensively and who spoke at least two languages, this girl from the country was a simple and naive foreigner who had no place in this exclusive house of learning. But as the weeks went by, they soon realized that Heidi's warm and loving presence in the school touched and affected each and every one of them. Quite unknown to Heidi, had there been a secret popularity contest at the end of term, Heidi would have been voted a clear winner. Academically, Heidi's progress had been less than spectacular, though the teachers saw great promise for the future. But her smile, personality and honest good sense had touched all hearts.

The school driveway was now almost deserted, and Lisl was the last to leave. A smart limousine was waiting, its engine running, as Lisl ran to Heidi and Elizabeth for her last goodbyes.

"I wish I could take you home with me," cried Lisl, kissing both Heidi and Elizabeth.

"Have fun, Lisl," said Elizabeth.

"But don't eat too much," Heidi advised, smiling.

"I'm already macraméing gifts for next Christmas," responded Lisl. "See you in January."

Heidi and Elizabeth waved as Lisl stepped into the car. The limousine roared down the driveway, with Lisl waving from the back window. Then all was quiet. Heidi and Elizabeth stood for a moment gazing at the car as it drove through the main gates and disappeared from view. They were still standing on the steps when Junius approached, stamping his feet to keep warm. At the sound of his voice they both looked round.

"You girls better wait inside. It's a very cold day."

"We're not waiting for anybody," said Heidi.

Elizabeth added, "We're staying here for Christmas."

"Bet's father had to go to New York," Heidi explained.

"I did ask him why we couldn't go with him," interposed Elizabeth.

Junius scratched his head. "But it was easier to let you stay here . . ." he mused.

Heidi looked at Junius as she gave a perfect imitation of Madame Lemay. "If only Madame had said: 'Herr Wyler, I'm sorry, but it is quite impossible for the girls to stay at the school.'"

"But she didn't say that—because it wasn't impossible," Elizabeth broke in.

Junius scratched his head again. "Maybe it could be . . ." was all he said. Junius paused for a moment, then stomped up the steps and into the building.

Madame Lemay had been working busily in her office when her concentration was broken by a sharp knock on the door. Junius entered and walked right up to her desk. He talked rapidly for several minutes. Madame Lemay looked up at him with surprise and alarm.

"I was not advised that the furnaces were to be repaired."

"I didn't think it concerned you, Madame, till I heard the students were staying over." Junius's tone changed from excitement to respect.

"That was a last-minute accommodation for Herr Wyler."

"There'll be no heat, except in my quarters, for

three or four days, at least," said Junius, almost triumphantly.

"All right. Certainly the furnaces must be repaired. Thank you, Junius—you may go."

Junius grinned to himself and made for the door as Madame Lemay reached for the telephone.

Two days before Christmas, the Wyler-Dietrich office was extremely busy. Mady was at her desk, typing furiously, every so often looking up apprehensively at Dan Wyler's closed office door. She stopped typing as Dan Wyler came out. He was dressed in a heavy overcoat, wearing a hat, and carrying a briefcase.

Dan stopped for a moment by Mady's desk, reaching in his pocket to check his passport and airline tickets, which Mady had delivered to him a few minutes earlier. Dan could hardly believe his eyes. He seemed completely baffled. "Why three airline tickets?"

Mady fussed with her typewriter ribbon and, without looking up, said deliberately, "You're not traveling alone."

"Mady—"

"The girls couldn't stay at the school. There's no heat there. Oscar's on holiday and they can't be left in the apartment alone."

The significance of Mady's words quickly dawned on Dan, but he still resisted their implication. "Some other arrangement must be made."

"They'll meet you at the airport. They're so excited." Mady was flushed but exhilarated by her unauthorized decision.

"I should fire you," said Dan in an exasperated manner.

"I have no regrets," said Mady complacently.

Dan looked at his secretary with a mixture of admiration and bewilderment, then with a shrug of his shoulders turned away.

"Fröhlich Weihnacht, Herr Wyler," Mady called after him.

Dan stopped and, returning to the desk, planted an efficient kiss on Mady's forehead.

"Fröhlich Weihnacht, Mady."

Mady watched Dan Wyler leave. For a few moments she sat motionless as if in a daze, her hands resting on the typewriter keys.

Chapter XIX
THE NEW WORLD

Heidi had been at Kloten airport once before, but that was on a Sunday afternoon with Mady and Bet, when they had watched the planes from the airport roof. Today everything was different. The crowds of passengers and well-wishers, the stacks of brightly labeled luggage, the porters hurrying with their trolleys, the cars, the lines at the ticket counters, the general hum of conversation over the shouts and the shrill whistles of the taxi drivers and, beyond, the muffled roar of the jets as another plane took off into the mystery of the clouds. Everything was so overwhelming to Heidi as she clutched Elizabeth's hand.

They were standing at the main departure gate with the Nordstrom chauffeur as Dan Wyler drove up. Dan thanked the driver for looking after the two girls, then hustled them to the check-in counter.

Security and immigration checks went by quickly, and after a short bus ride to the plane, during which Heidi insisted on standing and unsuccessfully trying to reach the overhead leather strap, they were seated in the first-class cabin of the Swissair 747 bound for New York. Heidi sat by the window, with Elizabeth next to her. Dan Wyler sat across the aisle, immersed in the financial pages of the Zurich newspaper. Heidi was fascinated by the lighted sign above her head telling her to fasten her seat belt. Heidi remembered once seeing belts like this on the ski lift near Bad Ragaz, but that was different. She smiled, fumbling with the heavy catch. Elizabeth helped her, giggling. "That's so you don't hit the ceiling."

Heidi looked up apprehensively, hoping flying was not that dangerous. Then, quickly taking hold of Elizabeth's hand, she assured her she was fine and everything was wonderful. The two girls smiled at each other.

As the plane taxied across the airfield and took off with a powerful roar, Heidi's nose was pressed against the window.

"Bet, look!" Heidi pointed down and Elizabeth stretched over her to get a better view. Down below, far below, a tiny village nestled in the mountains, the little chalets minute dots on the green-and-white slopes.

"Bet—it's a little town—like Dörfli. And that must be a lake. Bet, we're higher than the mountains. I'm looking down at the mountains!"

"If you don't look out the window, you'll forget you're on a plane," said Elizabeth, with the air of a seasoned traveler.

"But I don't want to forget. I don't want to miss anything."

And for a long while Heidi stared out of the window, at the clouds, and between the clouds at a glimpse of mountain, and again more clouds. Then her head nodded and her eyes closed as the dull whine of the engines lulled her to sleep.

Dan looked over at the two sleeping girls, then returned to his work, an open briefcase with papers littering his seat tray. It was getting dark, and Dan switched on his overhead light. The plane droned on over the deep Atlantic.

It was almost dark when the jetliner circled, preparing to land at Kennedy Airport, New York. Two hours earlier, the girls had awoken to the sounds of activity from the kitchen area. Stewardesses had been moving down the aisles, laying tables in preparation for a meal. Heidi wondered whether it would be supper or breakfast. She looked out of the window into the grey sky, puzzling as to whether it was day or night outside. It had seemed a long night, and she had expected to wake up to morning, but according to Elizabeth's watch, which had been adjusted to New York time, it was only late afternoon. When the tray was placed in front of Heidi, she knew this could not be breakfast, but must be something very special, with all the crystal and silver and a beautiful linen napkin. Heidi stroked the handle of one of the silver knives when her eye caught a large red carnation resting in the corner of the tray against a butter dish. She picked up the flower, kissing it and inhaling the rich scent. Poor flower, she thought, so far up in the sky and away from home, it must be thirsty. She thrust the carnation into her water glass. Elizabeth giggled, then, as if to reassure Heidi, she said, "That's very pretty—but I prefer the mountain flowers."

"All flowers are pretty," she said, twirling the carnation round in her glass. A stewardess interrupted them as she placed large bowls of salad on their trays. Heidi had become used to salad at school, but it always reminded her of her pet rabbit and how he would have enjoyed such a treat. Dish followed dish, and although neither girl did justice to the meal, they both enjoyed the attention and service given by the stewardess, who had given Heidi such a friendly "Grützi" when she had boarded the plane.

The tables had barely been cleared when the loudspeaker announced that they were approaching Kennedy Airport, and all seat belts must again be fastened.

Heidi giggled to Elizabeth as she buckled her belt.

"We didn't really need them, and nobody hit the ceiling! But they're very thoughtful, and all these people are so kind."

Elizabeth nodded. "Look out the window, Heidi —we're almost in New York."

Through the dark grey mist, Heidi could see nothing but lights. In the distance she could see water and, growing straight upwards like dark reeds in a pond, hundreds of slender buildings, all twinkling in the night and brighter than the mountain stars. Lights, lights, lights, as far as she could see.

The plane touched down, the brakes squealed, and the jetliner shuddered to a stop.

Dan Wyler immediately took charge and guided the two girls out of the plane, down endless corridors, through customs and immigration, where Mady had supplied special papers for Heidi, and on to the baggage claim area.

Soon they were all in the limousine Dan had ordered and were winding their way towards Manhattan. Dan pointed out to Heidi the silver towers in the distance, which was their destination.

"Manhattan looks like an enchanted forest," Heidi remarked.

The limousine crossed a bridge and entered the labyrinth of streets and giant skyscrapers that Dan told her was midtown Manhattan. They moved slowly in an endless stream of cars. The traffic was overwhelming.

The limousine moved slowly down Park Avenue.

"A famous street, like the Bahnhofstrassel" whispered Elizabeth.

The car swung left across the avenue and stopped outside a tall building.

"Here we are," said Dan. "This is the Waldorf Astoria."

A tall man in uniform opened the limousine door. Heidi noticed the doorman's name badge on his chest. "ERIC JENSEN," she read.

"Welcome to the Waldorf, Mr. Wyler," said

Jensen as another porter stacked up the luggage on the sidewalk. "I see you're going to have company this time. Welcome, young ladies—"

"Grützi," said Heidi, looking up at the doorman. "You're the tallest man I've ever seen."

Jensen chuckled. "Just wait till I get off my knees," he said, supervising the luggage.

Dan led the two girls through the large glass doors, up the thickly carpeted stairs and across the lobby to the reception desk.

Heidi was wide-eyed as, looking around, she nudged Elizabeth and whispered, "It's like a royal palace."

The two girls waited in the center of the lobby as Dan talked to the desk clerk. The assistant manager, Ray Krebs, was hovering in the background. On seeing Dan, he brushed away the desk clerk and put out his hand.

"Dan, am I relieved to see you," he said, shaking Dan's hand.

"Glad I could make it, Ray. I take it the situation in the kitchen hasn't improved."

Straightening his tie and coughing nervously, Krebs said, "Worsened—if that's possible. André's not only incapable of doing his own work, he's demoralizing everyone else."

"All right," said Dan. "Just give me ten minutes to get the girls settled, and we'll get to work."

Krebs nodded, took some keys from a rack and pushed a bell. "Front!" he called with authority.

A serious-looking young bellboy jumped up, taking the keys from Krebs. Dan collected Heidi and

Elizabeth and steered them to the elevators. The bellboy followed with the luggage.

In the elevator Heidi studied the bellboy, whose name, which she read from his badge, was "HAROLD." Harold wore thick glasses and Heidi hoped he could read the floor indicator correctly. She looked up at the young man.

"Grützi, Herr Harold," she said brightly.

Harold's attention was distracted from the elevator floor numbers. "Grützi?" he asked, "what's that?"

"That's how we say 'hello' in Dörfli."

"And where's whatever you said?" asked Harold.

"Switzerland," she replied.

"Oh, sure, Switzerland. I know. Tall mountains and," Harold pointed to Heidi, "short people."

They all laughed, even Dan, though he obviously had his mind on hotel problems. The elevator stopped and Harold motioned them forward, following with the luggage. They were shown into one of the Waldorf's best suites.

Heidi immediately ran round the rooms on a tour of inspection, clapping her hands. "Wunderbar," exclaimed Heidi as she saw the large bedroom leading off the sitting room, and the dressing room and bathroom.

Dan was standing by the door as Heidi and Elizabeth looked round the rooms, and Harold stacked their luggage. "I have the suite next door," said Dan. "After you unpack, you can wander around the hotel. Just don't get lost."

Heidi thought she might even get lost in their suite. She looked at Dan. "Maybe you should put bells on us—the way we do with our goats."

Harold smiled.

"When will we see you?" Elizabeth asked her father.

"I have to work out this problem with the chef. It's still quite early on New York time, so if you don't want to go to sleep, order anything you want from room service." Dan motioned to Harold, who followed him out to his suite next door.

Heidi and Elizabeth were alone. Alone in New York, in a suite at the Waldorf Astoria. With the departure of Dan Wyler and Harold, they both felt a little lost. Heidi plumped herself down in one of the easy chairs and looked at Elizabeth questioningly.

"What's 'room service'?"

Elizabeth, who was also feeling strange in these new surroundings, made an effort to assume the role of an experienced traveler.

"You just pick up the phone," she answered, "and ask for room service, and you can order anything."

"Anything?" Heidi was incredulous. "Home-baked bread, cheese, rösti and goat's milk? Anything?"

Both girls broke out laughing.

"Just try it," suggested Elizabeth, smothering her giggles.

Heidi strode to the phone determinedly, picking

up the receiver and listening. In a moment a polite, efficient-sounding woman answered. "May I help you?"

Heidi smiled at Elizabeth, who winked in encouragement.

"Grützi," said Heidi, addressing the anonymous operator.

There was a moment's pause. "I beg your pardon—" said the woman.

"Grützi," repeated Heidi, "that's how we say hello in my country."

The woman became friendlier. "Grützi," she said. "What can I do for you?"

Heidi was now much more relaxed and, carrying the phone to her chair, prepared herself for a chat with a newfound friend.

"I'd like just to talk to you. You sound so friendly and I feel you can help us."

"Why, thank you, dear—what can I do?"

"Well, we really want room service."

"Of course—" There was a pause, followed by a ringing tone. Elizabeth looked at Heidi with pride, and the two girls smiled and nodded to each other.

Chapter XX
AT THE WALDORF

Meanwhile, many floors below, a drama was developing in the busy kitchen of the great hotel. Chefs and helpers were frantically chopping, mincing, beating and stirring countless dishes laid out in rows on thick oak tables. The multitude of white-uniformed figures seemed in a frenzy to complete their various tasks. Steam was rising from a quantity of copper pots bubbling on vast ranges. The walls and overhead racks were laden with skillets, pans, knives and utensils of every conceivable kind. André Velu, recognized by all his fellow workers as one of the greatest chefs in the world, sat at a table, in the corner, seemingly oblivious to the hubbub around him. André was taking no part in the general activity. A passionate, volatile man by nature, considered by chefs throughout the world as a great artist—an opinion shared, incidentally, by André himself—he was now slumped across the table in an attitude of abject despair and depression.

Dan Wyler stood beside the despondent André,

pleading with him. "André," said Dan quietly, patting the chef on the shoulder.

André did not look up, but continued staring into space as he answered. "Dan, why are you here in this awful place?"

The two men had been friends for many years, and Dan had helped André become one of the stars of the culinary world after discovering him in a tiny restaurant behind the harbor at Cannes.

"I flew in from Zurich because I was concerned about you," Dan said to his old colleague.

For the first time, André turned to his friend. "*Mon ami*—do not be concerned about me. Concern yourself with all the primitives and incompetents who surround me, these bunglers who can't carry out the simplest of orders."

"Now, André, there are very good men on your staff."

André ignored Dan's statement, though he knew it was true. "If I could do it all alone," he said, "just me, just André, then it would be perfect."

"But you know that's impossible," Dan protested.

André was adamant. "Depend on another person —just one other person, and you're finished. So— André is alone. And André will stay alone!"

Dan's reply began to show his increasing impatience. "Now look, you're creating a very difficult situation."

At that moment, just behind them, a junior chef in charge of soufflés opened an oven door to inspect his creations. André looked up as the oven door

opened, the diversion making him raise his voice
to a scream.

"I suffer. I am hurt. Let everyone else know
pain, too."

André looked at the junior chef in disgust as the
oven door closed. Dan moved closer to André.

"I don't want anyone to suffer," he said quietly.
"Maybe you should take a few days off."

The junior chef had now placed a tray of his
soufflés on the corner of the table.

"I will not leave!" shouted André, striking the
table with his fist. A soufflé fell, and with each
further exclamation from André, accompanied by
a thumping of his fist, another soufflé deflated.
"This is my kitchen!" André cried. "Mine, mine,
mine! I've nothing else left; but this I will keep!"

The soufflé chef was, by this time, in despair,
almost rivaling André as he surveyed his ruined
handiwork.

"André—" pleaded Dan once more.

But André was now thoroughly aroused and,
jumping to his feet, grabbed two wicked-looking
chopping knives, brandishing them above his head.
He appeared to be threatening both Dan and the
junior soufflé chef.

"No more! Get out! Get out!" he screamed.

Both Dan and the soufflé chef took a rapid step
away from the maddened André.

"Out—out!" André repeated at the top of his
voice.

At this last outburst, Dan, realizing at least a
temporary defeat, turned on his heels and made

his way hurriedly past the busy white-coated work-ers, through the swinging doors and into the com-parative calm of a narrow corridor, leaving the turmoil of the kitchen behind him.

Heidi and Elizabeth had ordered room service to deliver food to their suite in an hour's time. Al-though it was late, and they were not really hun-gry, they both wanted to test this magic service where, by merely placing a phone call, anything they desired would be brought to them. Since neither of them was tired, they decided to explore the hotel before room service arrived. Their tour was delayed slightly because Heidi insisted on riding the elevator from the top to the bottom of the building twice before they both finally stepped out into the magnificent hotel lobby.

After an hour's wandering, Heidi decided that all the hotel staff were delightful people and the kindest and most helpful in the world. They ex-plored almost everywhere, though somehow or other missed the kitchen area. They did, however, renew acquaintanceship with the head doorman, Eric Jensen, who let them stand and watch the endless stream of taxis and cars draw up to and leave the main entrance. But there was a cold wind outside and they soon decided to find a warmer place of interest—the linen room—and the girls were spellbound by the thousands of square meters of neatly folded towels and sheets. They were happy to get a guided tour of the linen department by a cheerful maid, Teresa, and watched in awe as Teresa folded and stored the linens delivered from the laundry.

Their last visit was to the main telephone switchboard, because Heidi was determined to meet the woman who had connected her to room service. The woman's name was Nora, and Heidi liked her immediately. Nora patiently explained to the two girls the intricate workings of the massive hotel switchboard.

When at last they reached their suite, a waiter was already outside the door with a large trolley, laden with crystal, silver dishes, flowers and a small candelabra.

"I knocked," he explained, "and I thought you ladies must be asleep, but I didn't see the 'Do Not Disturb' sign."

"Oh, but we want to be disturbed. Come on in," said Heidi brightly, unlocking the suite door.

The waiter laid the table and, having lit the candles on the silver candelabra, bowed his way out. "*Bon appétit, m'amselles,*" he said, leaving the two girls sitting on either side of the table, facing more silver than Heidi had ever seen.

"How nice of him—what a kind man," said Heidi, carefully unfolding her linen napkin. Heidi lifted the heavy cover of a large engraved silver dish. In the center of the plate, lying alone on a white linen doily, was a square chunk of Swiss cheese. Both girls laughed as they divided the cheese between them.

"Just like Dörfli cheese," bubbled Heidi. But her gaiety soon faded, and a sad expression replaced her smile.

"You're thinking of Grandfather," said Elizabeth. Heidi nodded, her mouth full of cheese.

They finished their simple meal in silence. The joy and magic of the evening had vanished.

Later, when they were both lying in their large double beds, Heidi stretched over to turn off the reading light. As she turned the light switch, her hand accidentally touched a button on the radio built into the night table. Softly, Christmas carols whispered through the dark bedroom. Heidi lay on her back, looking at the ceiling, with its flickering reflections of a neon sign blinking from far out in the Manhattan sky. She did not immediately turn off the radio, but let the soft tones of the melody engulf her. "O Tannenbaum, O Tannenbaum." Heidi's eyes grew misty, and she was far away. It had been a long day, but sleep was still evading her. Tomorrow was Christmas Eve, and memories of past Christmases on the mountain flooded her mind. She could not recall her grandfather being a particularly religious man, but she could still see him on Christmas Eve, bringing out the old black leather book from the cupboard and settling himself in his rocker to read aloud the mystical story of the first Christmas. Heidi used to squat on the floor beside the old man, with her hands clasped round her knees, and listen to the words she now almost knew by heart. The Wise Men who followed a star, the child born in a manger because there was no room at the inn. Heidi always felt so sad that a baby had to born in a stable. She worried about it every time her grandfather told the tale, slowly but dramatically, in his deep old voice. Yet every year he sounded as though he were telling it for the first time, though Heidi sometimes saw him close the book as he spoke and still the rich words rolled on. "Unto us a child is born. Unto us a Son is given!" Heidi always brightened up at those words. How wonderful! "Unto us a Son is given." Heidi repeated the words in a whisper, and the picture of Grandfather, sitting in his rocker reading aloud, faded. But another picture took its place. A fir tree standing proudly by the Alm-hut fireplace, lighting up the room with its blazing candles. Every year her grandfather used to cut an especially fine tree and decorate it with candles and ornaments that he had bought at the general store in Dörfli. And every year it was supposed to be a surprise, although the lighting of the tree had become a traditional yearly custom. It was a secret joke between them. Heidi always saw her grandfather bring the tree into the Alm-hut, but she pretended not to notice. The surprise was when the old man lit the candles. It was at a different time each year. That was his little whimsy. Then, and only then, would the grandfather exclaim— "Look, Heidi! Look at the Tannenbaum!" And Heidi, gazing at the brightly lit tree and then at her grandfather, would exclaim—"It's beautiful, Grandfather, just beautiful." Then Heidi would run to the old man, jump on his lap and give him a big kiss. "Fröhlich Weihnacht, Grandfather." And Grandfather, in one of his rare outward displays of affection, would hug Heidi with a bear's grip. "Fröhlich Weihnacht—Heidi."

Visions of Christmas at the Alm-hut slowly dissolved, leaving only the flickering lights of Manhattan on the hotel ceiling. Heidi closed her eyes and was soon lost in sleep. The radio played softly.

Far away, thousands of miles across the Atlantic Ocean, beyond the barrier of the wild Savoy Alps and beyond to the valley of the Rhine, it was already Christmas Eve.

But in the dark cave, nestled in the rocky crags of the Falknis, towering over the valley, months, days and seasons were meaningless. Grandfather sat on his rough bed, wrapped in animal skins. To him, the world was a black nothingness.

The Wild Man crouched by the fire, rubbing his hands against the cold.

Grandfather was speaking, either to himself, to the world or to anyone who would listen. He didn't care. But his words echoed round the cave.

"I sit here and I think crazy things. Maybe when I fell that night I died, and this is the dream of death. Maybe I'm in Hell, and this is my punishment. To spend eternity not being able to see, with someone who isn't able to speak. It's crazy—and yet I know I'm alive. If only I had the strength to refuse food and water—and then it would be over. Finally over—"

Grandfather sighed deeply, wrapping the skins

closer round his shoulders. The Wild Man said nothing.

Beyond the cave the winter wind howled in the night.

Chapter XXI
CHRISTMAS EVE

Christmas Eve dawned brightly in New York. The snow clouds, which had threatened yesterday, had scurried southwest over the ocean. The winter sunshine gleamed on the concrete towers, and when the two girls awoke the suite was bathed in yellow light. Heidi woke first, then scrambled over to shake Elizabeth.

"It's late, Bet. Time to get up."

Heidi took a luxurious hot bath and, when it was Elizabeth's turn for the bathroom, Heidi again tried the magic of room service, ordering orange juice, rolls and coffee. Putting down the phone, she looked out of the window at the wondrous sight of the Manhattan skyline. She did not recognize many of the famous buildings, although she remembered seeing a picture of the United Nations building in a magazine. She was still admiring the view when Elizabeth, wrapped in a towel, came out of the bathroom. Elizabeth seemed sad.

"Bet—what is it?" asked Heidi.

"I wish we'd stayed at school. At least Junius

cares about us." Elizabeth slumped down in a chair.

"But we're in New York—with your father."

"What do you mean, with him? We haven't seen him since we got here." Elizabeth was disconsolate.

"He's doing his job," Heidi assured her.

"I knew it wouldn't work. I wanted to believe that somehow I'd finally spend Christmas with my father. But look at us, we're here all alone."

Heidi was her usual cheerful self. "We're not alone. This hotel's full of nice people."

"Who don't know we exist," Elizabeth interrupted. "And if they did, they wouldn't care."

"Some of them know and most of them care. There's Harold the bellboy, Herr Jensen the doorman, Nora Ryan at the switchboard, and that nice waiter—" Heidi did not finish naming all her hotel friends, as she had picked up the phone on a sudden impulse. She dialed "O." "Grützi," she said as she recognized Nora's voice.

"Grützi, Heidi. What can I do for you?"

"Frau Ryan, my friend Bet is feeling lonely and homesick."

"Well, we can't have that, can we?" said Nora reassuringly. Heidi listened to her for several minutes, and then put down the phone.

"Get dressed, Bet, quickly. We're going out," cried Heidi exultantly. Elizabeth obeyed, running to the bedroom. Heidi put on her coat.

"Hurry up, Bet," she called.

Just as they were leaving, they met Dan Wyler returning to his suite next door. He looked tired and explained briefly the problems he was having with his head chef.

"Got to get a few hours sleep," said Dan, unlocking his door, "have a good day." He disappeared into his room, leaving the two girls standing in the corridor. They looked at each other. Elizabeth glanced towards her father's closed door and with a shrug followed Heidi to the elevator.

A few minutes later, both Heidi and Elizabeth were down at the main entrance of the hotel. Heidi, seeing the doorman, ran over to him.

"Herr Jensen—Frau Ryan said to come down to see you and—"

"Well, well, of course," said Eric Jensen. "We can't have our two Swiss misses going home with no memories of New York but the inside of their hotel room, can we? Come on, then—I've only got an hour." With that, Eric Jensen grasped each girl by the hand and marched them off down Park Avenue. Heidi was ecstatic that her plan was working and every now and then gave a little skip and a jump. Even Elizabeth seemed happier now that someone was taking an interest in them.

As they walked down Park Avenue, Jensen kept up a nonstop commentary, pointing out places of interest and telling them stories, both historic and fanciful, about the city and its people.

"You know as much about New York as Mady does about Zurich," cried Heidi, looking up at the tall doorman. They all laughed.

When they reached the Plaza, Jensen insisted they all take a ride in one of the open-horse carriages that line that corner of Central Park. Heidi and Elizabeth readily agreed, and off they went spinning down Central Park South. An observer would have had difficulty deciding which of the three looked the happiest and proudest. Their ride over, Jensen told them of the next step in their plans.

"Now I'm going to take you to Rockefeller Plaza. There we'll meet Harold. You know Harold, he carried your bags last night. Then I've got to go back on duty, but Harold will look after you till you're ready for Mrs. Ryan." And Jensen bustled them into a taxi. Heidi and Elizabeth were both bewildered. Apparently Heidi's phone call earlier had put a whole day's tour plan into motion.

When they reached Rockefeller Plaza, Harold was waiting by the ice rink, his skates hanging round his neck.

"You're in good hands," said Eric Jensen, waving and disappearing into the crowd on Fifth Avenue. Harold quickly arranged skates for the two girls, and soon the trio had joined the other skaters and were circling round the rink. Heidi decided she'd never had such a good time in her life. Her face was flushed in the cool air as she spun a figure eight, encouraging the other two to follow her. Elizabeth did her best, as she was a fair skater, but Harold, who was obviously a keen but determined novice, spent a lot of time picking himself up off the cold and slippery ice. After a while Harold beckoned Heidi and Elizabeth to join him at the rinkside café, where he ordered hamburgers and Cokes.

"You're going to have some typical American food," he said, showing Heidi how to spread ketchup and relish on her burger. Heidi munched thoughtfully.

"That's really delicious," she said. "I'll have to get the Alpenrose to make these."

"The Alpenrose?" Asked Harold.

"Just another famous hotel we know," said Elizabeth, winking at Heidi.

When they had finished their lunch, they saw Nora Ryan waving to them from the street level above.

"Okay—there's your next guide," said Harold. "See you guys later."

Nora Ryan asked Heidi and Elizabeth what they'd like to do next, as she had two hours free. Nora suggested the Empire State Building or one of the several museums nearby. Looking at the crowd of shoppers and the brightly lit store windows on Fifth Avenue, the two girls agreed that what they'd really prefer would be to look at the New York shops.

"Fine," agreed Nora, taking their hands, "but hold on tight. I can't afford to lose you both."

Despite the throng on the streets they managed to stop and gaze in wonder at the many elaborate window displays and Christmas scenes with automatic moving figures. The girls stopped and gasped as each new storefront seemed more fantastic than the last. Heidi especially liked F.A.O. Schwarz, which Nora explained was the biggest toy shop in the world, and she couldn't help but stop to pat the large lifelike moving animals in the display. After exploring Schwarz, they went past St. Patrick's Cathedral to Saks Fifth Avenue department store, which they decided would be their last stop before returning to the hotel. As they moved down the aisles of the store, Elizabeth suddenly grabbed Heidi's arm and stopped.

"Listen," she cried. Somewhere, over the hum of the crowd, came the faint but distinct tinkling of a music box. They moved towards the sound and found a counter with dozens of brightly colored music boxes. Above the buzz and hubbub of the shoppers, they listened to the clear melody from a beautiful red and white box painted with Christmas trees. "O Tannenbaum." For a moment, listening to the familiar old tune, Heidi remembered the radio of the night before. But her attention was soon attracted by the other boxes, and she picked up one and then another. Turning one over, she showed Elizabeth the small printed tag and they both giggled. "Imported from Switzerland."

"What's the joke, girls?" the salesclerk asked curiously.

Nora explained hurriedly. "These two ladies are also imported from Switzerland."

"Oh, I see," said the clerk, as Elizabeth checked and listened to a number of boxes. One played the theme from *Doctor Zhivago*, another, "Frère Jacques" and another, "Twinkle, Twinkle Little

Star." Listening to this last music box brought tears to Elizabeth's eyes.

"What is it, Bet?" asked Heidi anxiously.

"My mother always used to give Father a new music box for Christmas. He must have dozens." Elizabeth continued to listen, holding the music box to her ear. "Whenever I hear a music box or that tune, I think of Christmas mornings and her— in the old days. Heidi, I'd like to buy this for my father. What do you think?"

"I think it's a splendid idea," agreed Heidi.

When the three left the store, Elizabeth was clutching a small package, neatly gift wrapped with ribbon and a Christmas bow.

Back at the hotel, after thanking Nora for a wonderful shopping expedition, Heidi and Elizabeth returned to their suite, and found a surprise when they opened the door. A Christmas tree stood in the middle of the floor. Harold was on his hands and knees decorating the tree, with Teresa, the maid from the linen room, helping to place a silver star on the top branches.

Heidi and Elizabeth stood there, speechless.

Harold looked up from his work. "It's not too good a tree—but it's the best we could find," he apologized.

"It's wonderful, just wonderful," exclaimed Heidi, clapping her hands.

"I know where I can find some lights," said Teresa, moving to the door. Before she could leave, Heidi rushed up to her, giving her a big hug. Then

Heidi ran to the tree and kissed the surprised Harold on the forehead.

"You're the most wonderful people in the world," said Heidi, looking at Harold and Teresa with admiration.

"And that's the most beautiful tree," added Elizabeth.

After Teresa had returned with a string of lights, which Harold carefully added to the tree, the two hotel workers left for their other duties, wishing Heidi and Elizabeth a "Merry Christmas." The suite was still. The two girls sat on the floor gazing at the tree in silence. It was a lovely Christmas Eve.

Some hours later, Teresa was back in the suite turning down the beds. Though normally only in the linen room, she had been given extra duties during the holiday season, and welcomed the chance to see the girls again. Heidi and Elizabeth followed Teresa into the bedroom. Pulling back the bed covers, Teresa asked, "How did your dad like the tree?"

"He hasn't seen it yet," answered Elizabeth sadly.

Heidi explained, "He's still trying to get that chef to do his job."

"That big baby," said Teresa, folding a cover. "If André was a man, he'd either forget that silly wife of his or go to France and get her."

Heidi looked surprised. "His wife is in France?" she asked.

Teresa, who obviously enjoyed a little hotel gossip, explained, "Oh, they had a lover's quarrel, and off she goes." Teresa raised her arms, snapping her fingers as though the chef's wife had vanished into thin air. Then she continued, more confidentially, "They're both hurting, but neither wants to make the first move. Mrs. Ryan says he starts to call her two to three times a day, but just as he's getting through—bang—he hangs up." Teresa snapped her fingers again. Finger snapping, Heidi noticed, was Teresa's favorite way of dramatizing her words. Teresa smoothed down the beds and on her way out stopped for a moment for another look at the Christmas tree in the living room, sparkling with lights. She nodded her approval. "That's really one of the prettiest trees I've ever seen. Merry Christmas, girls!"

"Merry Christmas!" called Heidi and Elizabeth.

No sooner had Teresa left than Heidi ran to the phone and called her friend Nora Ryan.

"Grützi, Mrs. Ryan. Do you have the phone number in France for Chef André's wife?"

Elizabeth watched Heidi in amazement as Heidi listened to the phone for several minutes, saying nothing, but nodding, apparently in agreement with what she was hearing. Heidi put down the phone.

"Come on, Bet—we're going down to see Mrs. Ryan—hurry."

In the depths of the hotel in the main kitchen, the staff, in contrast to the night before, were going through their duties in a mechanical manner.

Everyone seemed to be halfhearted in his work. André was slumped on a stool, surrounded by pots and pans. The phone by his elbow rang shrilly. André jumped, started to reach for the phone, then hesitated. The ringing continued, and with a grimace, André picked up the receiver.

"Allo," he grunted.

"I have a call for André Velu," said Nora Ryan. There was a pause—then he heard Nora continue. "One moment—go ahead, France." The line was not clear, and for several seconds all André could make out were crackles and a distant buzzing. Then he heard someone talking faintly over the background interference.

"André?"

The head chef was suddenly alert.

"Marie, oh *ma chérie*! I have prayed for this to happen."

The voice across the Atlantic was clearer now.

"*Et moi*, André. I do miss you so—"

André became excited. "I am a crazy man without you—I am destroying myself. Please, Marie, *chérie*, come back, come back—"

As André was speaking, on another floor of the hotel, at the busy switchboard, Nora, wearing her headset, was reporting the progress of the call in sign language to Heidi and Elizabeth standing beside her. Watching Nora's expression, the girls were overflowing with nervous excitement. When Nora finally put down the headset, raising both thumbs as a signal of victory, Heidi and Elizabeth jumped in the air, first hugging each other, and then Heidi flung her arms around Nora's shoulders.

"We did it, we did it!" Heidi cried joyfully.

The two girls triumphantly returned to their suite. Their elation and exuberance had faded when an hour later they were sitting silently staring at the Christmas tree, and still there was no sign of Dan Wyler.

As every minute passed, Elizabeth became more disconsolate. Heidi did her best to cheer up her friend.

"He'll be here soon, Bet." But Elizabeth only shook her head. The silence was suddenly broken by a knocking on the door. Heidi jumped up, opened the door, and in walked Elizabeth's father.

"Herr Wyler!" cried Heidi, with excitement and relief in her voice.

"I'm sure you were waiting for Santa Claus," said Dan, smiling.

"We were hoping it was you," said Elizabeth.

Dan Wyler settled himself on the sofa. He appeared much more relaxed. The nervous fatigue of that morning had gone. He sounded like a man who had undergone a mental and physical struggle that was now over. He spoke quickly and calmly.

"I was prepared to spend the night in the kitchen, but André did a complete turnaround. It was unbelievable. André embraced everybody, apologized to me and even to the junior chefs. Whatever happened, I don't know—but the crisis seems to be over."

Heidi and Elizabeth exchanged knowing smiles. "That's wonderful, Father," said Elizabeth.

Dan looked around the room.

"Did you two fix the tree?" he asked.

"We had a lot of help," said Heidi.

Dan had, by now, seen the little packages beside the tree and admitted, "I'm sorry, but I just haven't had the time to buy presents."

"That's all right, Father—you've already given us your present—just by being here."

Dan looked relieved, "Well, when do I get my present?" he asked.

"Heidi—you go first," prompted Elizabeth.

Heidi reached for one of the packages. Even Elizabeth had not seen Heidi's gift, as she'd been busy looking at dresses with Nora Ryan when Heidi had slipped off on her own into a little shop on Fifth Avenue. Dan unwrapped his present as Heidi explained, "I thought that since you travel so much you could use this. It's a thermometer, barometer and compass—all in one."

"Thank you, Heidi. It's just great. I'll never be lost in Shanghai again."

Elizabeth nervously gave her father the wrapped music box. "Merry Christmas, Father."

Both girls watched him apprehensively as he undid the wrapping. When he lifted the music box from the gift wrap he froze, staring at it motionless, his expression one of sadness and dismay. Slowly, as if afraid of the result, he opened the music box lid. The first notes of "Twinkle, Twinkle Little Star" broke the awkward silence in the room. Dan quickly closed the lid and, getting to his feet, banged the music box down on the table.

"I'm sorry you did this—Elizabeth."

Heidi looked at Elizabeth, who was gazing at her father, wide-eyed and trembling.

"What did I do, Father? I'm sorry—please don't go."

Dan looked round the room like a trapped animal, seeking escape from a cage, and headed towards the door.

"I have to make arrangements for our flight home tomorrow. Get a good night's sleep. It will be a long, tiring day." And he was gone.

"Oh!" Elizabeth cried out as though in sudden pain and snatched the music box from the table. In a fit of frustrated rage and grief she was about to smash the box on the floor when Heidi grabbed her.

"Don't, Bet, don't."

"He hated it. He hates me!" Elizabeth was hysterical.

"No, Bet—he doesn't. Really he doesn't."

"But you saw the way he looked at me."

As Elizabeth spoke, Heidi, with an arm round her friend, led her gently back to her chair.

"He was thinking of your mother, Bet," said Heidi softly. Elizabeth was calmer, but her lips quivered as she spoke.

"He loved her—so why does he hate me for making him think of her? He just can't stand to have me near him. I don't ever want to see him

again—ever." At this, Elizabeth again lost control
and broke down sobbing.

"Bet, please." Heidi stroked Elizabeth's head,
making every effort to soothe her. "Don't cry,
please don't cry. Somehow it will work out. I know
it will."

Elizabeth clung to Heidi, her sobbing racking
her body with convulsions.

In the dimness of the large suite, lit only by the
glow from the Christmas tree, the two girls sat
huddled together. It was the last fading hours of
Christmas Eve.

In the hotel kitchen, many floors below, tired
chefs and busboys were wearily cleaning and tidying up, restoring the kitchen to some semblance of
order after hours of frenzied activity. An ex-
hausted but triumphant André was sprawled on a
stool. Across the table from him sat Dan, his head
in his hands, looking dejected and deeply troubled.
André spoke exultingly, raising his voice to be
heard over the clatter of pans.

"A triumph, my dear Dan. An absolute and total
triumph for André. The fortunate people who
dined here tonight—will never forget. I surpassed
even myself. And it was all thanks to you. You are
so wise and understanding—"

"That's a matter of debate," Dan said dully.

"You come, you listen and observe," continued
André. "You know what it is that overcooks André's St. Jacques and curdles André's sauces. So
what do you do? You play . . . Cupid!"

Dan looked up, questioningly. "Cupid?"

"Oh, yes—we know your trick, Marie and I. How you ended our stupid quarrel. When she hears my voice, and I hear hers, all the pride, stubbornness —it's all gone. Instead—joy and happiness." André clapped his hands.

"You mean you called Marie?" asked Dan incredulously.

"Aha! You know I didn't. And she didn't call me. But, *voilà*, there we are on the phone together. All is well, and she comes back to me."

"Well, congratulations," said Dan, not comprehending how the transformation of André had been effected, but immensely relieved that the problems of the temperamental chef appeared over.

"Love . . . " said André philosophically. "Love is a terrible force. It is bad when you offer love, and the other, she will not take your love. But you know a man feels even worse when someone holds out to him a gift of love, and because he's too blind or proud or selfish, he rejects it. Ah—that is terrible."

"Terrible," Dan repeated, jumping to his feet. André looked after him, wondering, as Dan hurried from the kitchen.

Back in his own suite, Dan quietly opened the connecting door and tiptoed into the girls' sitting room. The room was dark except for the lights from the Christmas tree. The bedroom door was open and he could see the girls were sleeping. Elizabeth seemed restless, turning in her sleep, and even in the dim light, he could see her troubled face, frowning as if from a bad dream. Dan took the music box from the table, wound it and opened the lid. Softly the melody filled the room. Holding the music box, Dan looked down on Elizabeth with a loving smile. Elizabeth opened her eyes.

"Father!" she cried, awakening Heidi.

"Elizabeth—thank you," said Dan, sitting on the edge of her bed.

"Oh—Father." Elizabeth sat up as Dan took her in his arms. The music box continued to play.

"I was afraid you never wanted to see me again—" said Elizabeth, snuggling against her father.

"I want to see you more and more. I want to be a father again—if you'll let me."

Heidi sat up in bed, smiling, as Elizabeth hugged him even more tightly.

"Fröhlich Weihnacht, Elizabeth," said Dan.

"Fröhlich Weihnacht, Father."

Dan looked across at Heidi. "Fröhlich Weihnacht, Heidi."

"Fröhlich Weihnacht, Herr Wyler."

Dan gently laid Elizabeth down, and, tucking in the covers, gave her a warm kiss. He quietly returned to his suite next door. The last notes from the music box faded, and all was still.

Lying in the hushed dark, as waves of sleep swept over her, Heidi, through half-closed eyes, was dimly aware of the blurred outline of the Manhattan skyline. Slowly the dark skyscrapers dissolved into mountain peaks. Heidi sighed and was lost in sleep.

Chapter XXII
CHRISTMAS DAY

Outside the cave, the wind was roaring over the deep blanket of snow that covered the mountain and stretched into the valley below. Within the cave two figures crouched before the fire, eating. As Grandfather, in his world of darkness, scraped the last spoonful from his plate, the Wild Man refilled it from a copper pot hanging over the fire.

"Danke schön." After a pause, Grandfather mused aloud. "I wonder if Christmas has passed."

"Christmas!" answered the Wild Man bitterly.

Grandfather was so surprised to hear his companion speak that he let his plate drop and clatter to the floor. Groping, he retrieved the plate, and managed to scoop up most of the lost meal. Now that the Wild Man had spoken, he did not want to lose the opportunity of making conversation.

"Not your favorite time of year?" he asked.

"Peace on earth and good will to all men," the Wild Man quoted mockingly.

"Umm," grunted Grandfather. "That was the message."

The Wild Man spoke haltingly, his words coming slowly and dropping like stones in a deep pond.

"Christmas—Nineteen Forty—the last Christmas."

"For you?" asked Grandfather.

The Wild Man did not answer immediately. His lips moved silently, and his face became contorted, as though thoughts were rushing through his mind and he could not find words to express them. His confusion was lost on Grandfather—to whom all was blackness, but eventually the Wild Man broke the silence with a stream of tumbling words.

"We lived . . . in Rotterdam. My mother, my father, brother Jan, sister Franca and my brother Victor. My wife . . . Ilse . . . and our new baby. All together for Christmas. All together . . . and then the bombs fell. And the fire came. The fire . . . dear God . . . the fire."

The Wild Man was shaking and could hardly continue.

"I lived," he said. "Only me. Why?"

Grandfather didn't know what to say. He muttered, "Rotterdam's a long way from here."

The Wild Man, controlling himself, continued, "As a boy, my family brought me to these mountains on holidays. I don't know how I found my way back here. But I did. I was alone and I stayed alone."

"Until you took me in," said Grandfather. "I know a little of what you felt that Christmas in Rotterdam. I've also been hurt, and I've also hated.

But hate can keep you alive, and despite everything, I'm thankful for these last years. For I've been given something more."

"You're thinking of the child," said the Wild Man softly, "the little girl."

"Wherever Heidi is, she's better off with me as I am . . . and will be . . . " Grandfather's words trailed off. The Wild Man did not answer, staring vacantly into the fire.

On this Christmas Day, in a dark cave hidden from the world in snow and rocks, two men crouched in silence, lost in their own thoughts.

In the first-class cabin of a Swissair jet cruising swiftly across the Atlantic, Heidi and Elizabeth had just finished an elaborate Christmas dinner. Elizabeth sat next to the window, as Heidi had insisted they take turns. The stewardess removed their trays, and Dan, across the aisle, took out a novel from his briefcase.

Elizabeth turned to Heidi and fondled a gold charm of the Statue of Liberty, strung on a gold chain around her neck. Heidi smiled back, displaying an identical gold charm and chain.

"Wherever in the world we go with Father, we can add a new charm."

Heidi giggled. "In that case, we'll have to visit a new place each time," she whispered.

Dan looked up from his book. "We're not home from this trip, Elizabeth, and you're already thinking of the next one."

"Just like you, Father," laughed Elizabeth.

"Heidi—are you all right?" asked Dan.

"I'm fine, Herr Wyler."

"No, she isn't fine," interjected Elizabeth.

"Bet!" said Heidi in a scolding tone.

"She's homesick for Dörfli," explained Elizabeth.

Dan put down his book. "Of course—I understand. Heidi, how would you like to visit your friends there before you and Elizabeth go back to school?"

Heidi gasped, her mouth and eyes opening wide. "Could we, could we really?" she cried.

"You can count on it," said Dan firmly.

Chapter XXIII
THE DISCOVERY

Beneath their winter mantle, the villages of Maienfeld and Dörfli and the mountains were at peace. Though the sun shone through the haze beyond the jagged mountain range, casting giant shadows into the valley below, the whole countryside slept in the magic stillness of winter.

Above Dörfli, however, at the Langes' farm, there was unusual activity. Peter, Heidi and Elizabeth were playing with the goats in the farmyard, watched by Peter's parents who, with Dan Wyler and Mady, were standing by the porch. Schneehöpli was nuzzling Heidi ecstatically.

"You see, she remembers you," said Peter.

"Of course, she does," exclaimed Heidi.

"She doesn't remember me from one day to the next," Peter grumbled. Heidi and Elizabeth both laughed.

"Poor Peterli," said Heidi, consoling him.

At the farmhouse door the others were in deep conversation.

"Heidi does well with you," said Jacob, looking at the playing children as he puffed his pipe.

"Heidi does well anywhere," answered Dan.

"Peter misses her. We all do," said Brigitte.

"But it's good she has a home with you, Herr Wyler," added Jacob.

Mady spoke quietly, "She still believes her grandfather will come back."

Jacob looked up towards the Falknis. "The mountains have taken him and that's the way Wilhelm would have wanted it."

"You don't think there's any chance?" asked Dan.

Jacob shook his head. "It's been a hard winter. An old man up there—maybe blind—" Jacob sighed and with the others turned to watch Heidi playing with the goats.

Peter was questioning Heidi. "Did you come back to see me or the goats?"

"Both."

"I want to hear about Zurich and New York—and how it feels to fly in a jet."

"We'll tell you," said Heidi, "but now I want to go up to Grandfather's house."

"Nothing's changed there."

"But I want to see it," persisted Heidi.

"The snow's very deep, even on the path," warned Peter.

But Heidi had made up her mind, and was trudging towards the trail. "I'm going anyway," she said.

"She still gets her way—same as always," muttered Peter, who, with Elizabeth, started to follow Heidi.

Dan and Mady, seeing the children leave, bade their farewells to the Langes and set off up the mountain after them.

When they reached the Alm-hut, it looked desolate and forlorn, half buried by the snow drifts. They headed towards the door, down the path Peter had cleared the week before. Heidi pushed the door with all her might, but it refused to open, ice and snow binding the heavy hinges. Dan put his shoulder to the old wood, and with a heave, the locks creaked and the door swung inwards.

Inside, the stube felt cold and looked dark and deserted. Peter, removing his mittens, blew on his hands, fumbled with a match box and lit the oil lamp. As the flame from the lamp grew, Heidi looked around slowly. Nothing had changed. Everything—almost everything—was as she remembered it. She looked at the empty rocker. The rug was there, just as she had folded and left it. Heidi gingerly tipped the rocker with one finger, and the old chair swung back and forth with its familiar squeak. Heidi suddenly grabbed the back of the rocker to stop the movement. She gripped the chair until her knuckles whitened as tears streamed down her cheeks.

"Heidi—" pleaded Mady.

"I wish I hadn't come back," Heidi gasped between her sobs. "I was wrong. Everybody else was right. Grandfather is dead. He's dead." Heidi was forcing out the words. "And I'm never going to see him again. It must be true. Why can't I believe it?

Why do I keep telling myself he's alive and he'll come back to me? Why do I feel that?"

Peter was staring out of the window as the others stood by Heidi. Mady put her arm around the sobbing girl.

Dan spoke quietly. "Heidi—when we lose someone we love very much, we keep that person alive in our hearts. There's nothing wrong with that." Dan looked at Elizabeth and then at Mady. "Nothing wrong at all as long as we don't shut out the people who are with us and still need us."

At the window, Peter stiffened, then turning to the others, put his finger to his lips. "Sh—sh—sh—" he whispered, beckoning to them. Dan wiped the frost from the panes, and they all peered out. There, by the shed, stood the Wild Man, with his hand shielding his eyes, looking towards them.

Dan, Mady and Elizabeth were startled and shaken by this strange figure standing in the snow.

"What is it?" cried Mady.

"The Wildenmann," said Heidi, with a tremor in her voice.

Peter cautiously opened the door, and the others followed him outside. The Wild Man, still about twenty meters away, stood motionless.

"He usually always runs away the second you see him," said Peter.

As if hypnotized, their eyes were all glued on the wild, long-haired figure as he slowly raised his hand and pointed at Heidi. Heidi stepped slowly forward towards the Wild Man.

"Heidi—wait!" called Dan after her.

"He won't hurt us," said Heidi calmly, taking a few more steps. The Wild Man turned away from the Alm-hut, moving up the mountain. Then he stopped and looked back.

"He wants us to follow him," called out Heidi, stepping carefully in the Wild Man's tracks. The Wild Man started to move across and up the slopes surprisingly quickly, following the same tracks he had made on his descent, tracks that zigzagged up the mountain and disappeared over the highest ridge.

The others were forced to follow in a straggly line as Heidi, trudging through the snow ahead of them, seemed determined to pursue this wild stranger.

Every now and then the Wild Man stopped and looked back, as if to make sure his followers were still in sight.

"Heidi," Dan called out after her. "Heidi, this is foolish and dangerous. He's leading us higher and higher." Dan gasped, and his breath formed icy clouds in the clear Alpine air.

"It'll be dark soon," panted Mady.

"I have to go with him," Heidi called back.

"Why?" asked Elizabeth desperately.

"You never wanted to follow him before," Peter added.

"I just have to," replied Heidi, continuing her determined trudge upwards after the weird fleeting figure.

They reached the rocky crags where Peter had

last chased the Wild Man, months before. But now the rocks were snow covered, and the going was treacherous. The Wild Man moved more slowly, stopping frequently as the party following struggled to keep pace. The Wild Man climbed up to a rocky ledge and waited again. Heidi scrambled onto the ledge with difficulty, Peter giving her a helping hand. The ledge was narrow, and the Wild Man had disappeared round a bend in the rocks. Heidi and Peter, hand in hand, inched their way along the narrow icy strip. Rounding the bend, they both stared. The Wild Man was nowhere in sight. Heidi leaned against the sheer rock face, overcome with exhaustion. Suddenly, as if alerted, she turned her head from the rocks and sniffed. There was smoke coming from behind a clump of snow-laden scrubby bushes. She nervously edged her way toward the puff of smoke and, seeing the animal skins hanging on the rock face, cautiously pulled them aside and entered the cave.

Grandfather was sitting on the edge of his bed and, hearing unfamiliar footsteps, looked blindly towards the entrance.

After the glare outside, it took a second or so for Heidi's eyes to become accustomed to the dark. Then the shadowy figure on the bed became real and she rushed towards him.

"Grandfather!" she cried.

"Heidi?"

She was in his arms, and they were hugging each other. The old blind man tenderly touched her hair and ran his hands over her face.

"Heidi!" was all he said, tears welling in his sightless eyes.

It was months later before Heidi could clearly recall the blur of events that followed on that winter evening. The long tiring trek down the snowbound path, the stop at the Langes' farm, the late-night visit to the Alpenrose and the long drive to Zurich. Looking back, she could only clearly remember the cave and her grandfather's face emerging from the shadows. Everything else was a dream, a weird, yet wonderful, dream. Her grandfather was alive. Her grandfather had come back to her.

Chapter XXIV
HAPPINESS
HAS NO TOMORROW

In a large private room in a Zurich hospital, Grandfather sat propped up in bed. Heidi stood beside him, holding the old man's hand very tightly. She looked at her grandfather adoringly. At the end of the bed stood a distinguished-looking man in a white coat consulting a chart and looking from the chart to his patient. On the other side of the room, surrounded by large vases of fresh flowers from Zurich's finest hothouses, sat Dan and Mady with Elizabeth.

Grandfather, staring into the blackness, had a firm and cheerful ring to his voice.

"So in Zurich they've even found a cure for old age."

Dan smiled at the old man's fine spirits.

"Herr Beck," said Dr. Lowe, "your blindness isn't caused by aging. All our tests show your eyes are in excellent shape for a man of your years."

"Just one weakness," Grandfather chuckled. "I can't see."

"There's pressure on the optic nerve," Dr. Lowe

continued. "We can operate to relieve that pressure, and you should see as well as ever."

"Nobody's taken a knife to me in sixty-seven years. I'm not sure I'm ready for it now."

"Dr. Lowe is the best," Dan assured him.

"I'm sure he is—" said Grandfather, before Heidi interrupted.

"Grandfather, please listen to me. Whatever you decide will be fine, because either way we'll go back to Dörfli and look after each other."

Dan gave Heidi a quick look. Grandfather reached out and gently touched Heidi's face.

"There are certain things I'd like to see again." The old man sighed. "Very well, Doctor, do your worst—or your best."

The next morning, everyone gathered in the same room to watch Dr. Lowe unwind the bandages bound tightly round Grandfather's head and over his eyes. They all watched expectantly.

"From what we hear, the monologue you delivered while they gave you the anesthetic was funnier than most comedy routines," said Mady.

"Everybody was laughing so hard, it's a wonder they managed to get their jobs done," added Dan.

"We'll find out soon whether they did," said Grandfather, as Dr. Lowe slowly removed each layer of gauze.

"You've got a job here anytime you want as executive in charge of morale. The patients are begging to be taken into the recreation room when you're there," said Dr. Lowe.

"Most dangerous disease in this whole place is self-pity," grunted Grandfather. "Everyone ought to be inoculated against it."

Heidi anxiously watched Dr. Lowe as each layer of gauze was carefully unwound.

"That must be the longest bandage in the world," she said.

"All this fussing and fretting. I just hope it's been worth all the trouble," muttered Grandfather.

Dr. Lowe removed the last layer and carefully peeled away the cotton pads covering the old man's eyes. Grandfather blinked. The room was a hazy blur, though it gradually came into focus. His lips slowly widened into a smile, as he distinctly saw Heidi's face before him. He looked at her lovingly.

"It was worth it!" he exclaimed as Heidi joyfully flung herself into her grandfather's outstretched arms. The others clustered around to congratulate the old man.

Grandfather mechanically thanked them for their good wishes, but his whole attention was on Heidi, and hers on him. This is their moment, thought Dan as he turned away. This is their time of happiness. Pausing at the door and taking a last look at the old man and the young girl gazing silently at each other in wonder, words Turgenev had written years before flashed through his mind:

Happiness has no tomorrow, it has no yesterday.
It remembers not the past, nor thinks of the
   future—

It is the present, not a day, but a single moment.

Yes, thought Dan, their happiness is now. This is their moment. He left the room and quietly closed the door.

"Extraordinary is the word to be used first, last, and repeatedly ... Anyone who meets Karen, even on paper, will postpone resigning from the human race."—*The Saturday Review*

☐ KAREN
Marie Killilea

As told by her mother, the inspirational story of Karen, who—despite a cerebral palsy handicap—learns to talk, walk, read, and write. Winner of the Golden Book Award and two Christopher Awards. $1.50 4376-40

☐ WITH LOVE FROM KAREN
Marie Killilea

Written in response to thousands of letters, this sequel to *Karen* tells of her growth from the age of seven into womanhood and relates more about the open friendliness and spiritual plenty of her family. $1.75 9615-32

DELL BOOKS

Outstanding Laurel-Leaf Fiction
for Young Adult Readers

□ **A LITTLE DEMONSTRATION OF AFFECTION**
  Elizabeth Winthrop $1.25
A 15-year-old girl and her older brother find themselves turning
to each other to share their deepest emotions.

□ **M.C. HIGGINS THE GREAT**
  Virginia Hamilton $1.25
Winner of the Newbery Medal, the National Book Award and
the Boston Globe-Horn Book Award, this novel follows M.C.
Higgins' growing awareness that both choice and action lie
within his power

□ **PORTRAIT OF JENNIE**
  Robert Nathan $1.25
Robert Nathan interweaves touching and profound portraits of
all his characters with one of the most beautiful love stories
ever told.

□ **THE MEAT IN THE SANDWICH**
  Alice Bach $1.25
Mike Lefcourt dreams of being a star athlete, but when hockey
season ends, Mike learns that victory and defeat become
hopelessly mixed up.

□ **Z FOR ZACHARIAH**
  Robert C O'Brien $1.25
This winner of an Edgar Award from the Mystery Writers of
America portrays a young girl who was the only human being
left alive after nuclear doomsday—or so she thought.

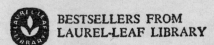

BESTSELLERS FROM LAUREL-LEAF LIBRARY